Without hesitation, I said the word. . . .

"Europe." I was so busy congratulating myself on my freshly found courage that I wasn't, wasn't at this moment, frightened.

"What!" shouted my father, and unless I'm mistaken my mother shouted it, too.

"Well," I said, knowing that after these next sentences left my mouth, "normal" would be a long time coming. "After much thought, I've decided to spend my own money—the thousand dollars that Grandmother and Grandfather gave me—going on a little tour of Europe. When I come back, you won't have to worry. I'll work part time and go to college part time. I won't be a burden! I'll pay my own way, I promise."

"Who ever heard of such a thing!" screamed my mother. "Who goes there? Nobody. Only soldiers to fight! Where does she get these ideas? She doesn't get them from me. So where?"

My father turned his attention and his comments toward her. "Calm down, Pearl! Now calm yourself down! What Patricia says she's going to do and what she actually does is a horse of a different color. She's going to Europe like I'm going to fly a kite."

"I am going," I said.

BOOKS BY BETTE GREENE

Get On Out of Here, Philip Hall
Morning Is a Long Time Coming
Philip Hall Likes Me. I Reckon Maybe.
A Newbery Honor Book
Summer of My German Soldier

Morning Is a Long Time Coming

Bette Greene

speak

An Imprint of Penguin Putnam Inc.

SPEAK

Published by the Penguin Group

Penguin Putnam Books for Young Readers,

345 Hudson Street, New York, New York 10014, U.S.A.

Penguin Books Ltd, 80 Strand, London WC2R ORL, England

Penguin Books Australia Ltd, 250 Camberwell Road, Camberwell, Victoria 3124, Australia

Penguin Books Canada Ltd, 10 Alcorn Avenue, Toronto, Ontario, Canada M4V 3B2

Penguin Books (N.Z.) Ltd, 182-190 Wairau Road, Auckland 10, New Zealand

Penguin Books Ltd, Registered Offices: Harmondsworth, Middlesex, England

First published in the United States of America by The Dial Press, 1978
Published by Puffin Books, a division of Penguin Putnam Books for Young Readers, 1999

This edition published by Speak, an imprint of Penguin Putnam Inc., 2003

10 9 8 7

THE LIBRARY OF CONGRESS HAS CATALOGED THE DIAL EDITION AS FOLLOWS:
Greene, Bette, date. Morning is a long time coming.
Summary: En route to Germany in search of the maternal love she never had,
eighteen-year-old Patty Bergen lingers in Paris and experiences her first
love affair. A sequel to "Summer of My German Soldier."
I. Title.
PZ7.G8283Mo [Fic] 76-42933 ISBN 0-8037-5496-5

Speak ISBN 0-14-130635-1

Printed in the United States of America

*To
Ruth Harmon
with reasons old
and
reasons new
but
with very good reasons*

Morning Is a
Long Time Coming

I · Jenkinsville

• 1 •

At the very moment Mrs. Turner began piano playing "Pomp and Circumstance," we graduates were given the nod to march on "with dignity." Our gym was divided for the occasion into two equal sections of people, most of whom overlapped their narrow metal folding chairs. Even though a gym is always a gym, the freshly strung crepe paper, along with the grandeur of Sir Edward Elgar's music, made it feel as though this was a place where something important was about to happen.

But unless I'm mightily mistaken, it didn't smell altogether different. For I could still smell the sour sweat of yesterday's athletes mingling with the soap and perfumed dusting powder of today's graduates.

"With dignity," I took my seat on the stage along with the other seventeen graduates of Jenkinsville High School (class of 1950) and began searching the audience for familiar faces. I knew practically everybody by sight and most of those I could hang a name onto. In the first row was the biggest landowner in all of Rice County, Arkansas, Mr. J. G. (for James Grady) Jackson and his wife. And next to them was Gussie Fields, who has been clerking in my father's store since even before her husband died.

And two rows behind Gussie were my father and mother, Mr. and Mrs. Harry M. (for Morry) Bergen, and my kid sister, Sharon (alias "the pretty Bergen girl" and I've even heard her referred to as "the sweet Bergen girl"). It's her black hair with just a hint of a widow's peak and her oval face that encourages people to say, "She's the spitting image of her mother." But the thing that really amazes me about Sharon is that she's the only one of us Bergens who seemed to be born in this world knowing exactly the right thing to say . . . and do.

And next to Sharon are my grandparents, Mr. and Mrs. Samuel Fried, who drove all the way from Memphis—forty miles—just to see me graduate.

Standing before the lectern, Superintendent Begley (he hates being called Coach Begley on formal occasions) was saying, "We're all real pleased and honored today to have as our commencement speaker one of Arkansas's up-and-coming young politicians. I take pleasure and pride in introducing to you all, State Representative Billy Bruce Stebbins."

A whole burst of welcoming applause greeted Mr. Stebbins, who folks say is a good bet to be governor someday. He's got about every qualification. A few years ago he was a star football player at the University, and later on he killed enough Germans to qualify as a genuine World War II hero. And frankly speaking, his poppa's money—the E. P. Stebbins of E. P. Stebbins & Sons, Ginners—won't hurt him. Not a bit.

With his back against us graduates and his face toward the guests, Billy Bruce Stebbins said that he was here today to bring a "personal message" to us graduating seniors. Right off, it struck me strange that anybody would say something personal with their back against you, but maybe that was only because he hadn't as yet reached the personal part.

"Six years ago, I was honored to have helped my country win their world war. I was there, ladies and gentlemen, when America called me. I was there when, with some help from our allies, this great Christian country of ours crushed the Axis powers to smithereens." He stuck his hands in his pockets in a way that showed that here at last was one man who'd never run from a fight.

"So you say we destroyed Hitler and Mussolini and that little Jap, Hirohito, so we've done our job. Nothing more to do!" The representative let his words lay uneventfully on his audience before suddenly bellowing out, "Well, is that what you all think?"

When the only sound that came back was the half-echo of his own question, he supplied, "No, ladies and gentlemen, that is not what right-thinking Americans led by real true

7

patriots like Senator Joe McCarthy and I believe. No, sir, not by a long shot! We Americans have got to stand like Christian martyrs against any and all those faceless, Godless *isms*. Fascism! Communism! And Socialism!"

He talked on and on about "alien ideologies" and how we Americans can't one bit more accommodate ourselves to the Russians than we could to the Germans. After a while, I noticed that some of the audience couldn't quite accommodate themselves to their chairs. Finally Mr. Stebbins half-turned from the audience toward us graduates, and I suspected that at long last our own "personal message" was coming right up.

"And so it is to you, the fine young men and girls of the 1950 Jenkinsville graduating class, that I want to personally tell, each and every one of you, that you MUST stand straight and tall against all Godless teachings in whatever form they are presented. And always remember this: All of us Christians represent God's very own reinforcements!"

The applause that sounded for his concluding remarks seemed a whole lot less vigorous than the applause that had welcomed him, but it's really hard to judge that sort of thing. So I could be mistaken.

After Coach—I mean Superintendent Begley thanked Mr. Stebbins, he introduced all of our class officers before turning the program over to our class president, Edna Louise Jackson, who gave a speech called "Jenkinsville High School, Farewell."

I told myself that just because I was passed over for class office is no reason for me to feel bad. After all I'm not really a leader like a president or a vice president has got to be.

But probably more important, I stand convicted of exactly

two crimes too many. The first charge is premeditated murder (after-the-fact—more than nineteen hundred years after the fact) of one Jesus Christ. Around here it is put more emotionally but less legally than that: "It was your people who killed our Lord."

Once the charge was even made in home ec class (of all places!) by our teacher, Mrs. Henrietta Gibbons. I raised my hand for recognition, and when it wasn't forthcoming, I stood up anyway and spoke my piece. "Mrs. Gibbons," I said in a voice trembling with fear and anger, "historians who don't seem to have quite so many axes to grind as Baptists say that it was Roman soldiers and not Jews who committed that crime!"

Anyway, I think I should have been elected class correspondent even though Juanita Henkins can spell and punctuate rings around me. Because her vocabulary is rudimentary compared to mine. And that's the truth!

It's not because I'm smart, it's only because words are my hobby. I would never want anybody from around here to know this, but I began studying Webster's Elementary School Dictionary when I was in the second grade. By the time I was in the sixth grade, I had graduated to Webster's Collegiate. And just last year my grandparents gave me Webster's Second International Dictionary. Unabridged and indexed and on genuine India paper. But then it oughta be. It cost twenty-five dollars!

But since my vocabulary isn't that noticeably great, I wouldn't have felt quite so upset about Juanita's being the class correspondent if I wasn't already a professional writer. I've written articles ranging from the Rice County Horse Show to the big Earle fire to the time last winter when Mr.

Conrad Ellis, legislative assistant to Senator Fulbright, spoke before the Jenkinsville Rotary Club.

Now my being a stringer for the *Memphis Commercial Appeal* may not exactly intimidate Pearl Buck, but at fifteen cents per column inch, it's not exactly nothing either. So would it have been so terrible for my classmates—far too much of a concession to this outsider—if they had allowed me to be class correspondent?

Besides having all the usual reasons for wanting one of the nine class honors, I guess I had still another reason. I needed an honor. Something that could erase from people's consciousness the memory of my second crime. Anything to blot out some of the dishonor!

I'm making too much of it. After all, spending nine weeks in a reform school didn't exactly make me a convict . . . did it? Besides, I truly believe that everybody has more or less forgotten all about that by now.

Sometimes though when I'm with somebody who seems especially nice, I want to ask them, personally speaking, if they ever think about that anymore. About what I did. But I always stop myself just in time because I know that it would only serve to remind people of the very thing that I want them to forget.

· 2 ·

SUDDENLY MRS. TURNER struck up a livelier, more spirited "Pomp and Circumstance" and we graduates marched triumphantly off the stage and out the door into the gym's dressing rooms. First thing Edna Louise Jackson and Juanita Henkins did was to bring out little mirrored compacts to apply fire-engine-red lipstick while Jimmy Wells shouted for quiet. "I have a big surprise for everybody!"

When the noise level dropped to almost bearable, Jimmy

announced in capital letters, "I have joined the United States Marines!"

Trying to become more of a member of the festivities than I actually felt, I sang out, "Anchors aweigh, my boy . . ."

Jimmy, looking for the world as though the one thing that he hadn't patience for was simple dumbness, stood incredibly straight and in a voice that was occasionally on key sang out, "From the Halls of Montezuma, to the shores of Tripoli. . . . We will fight our country's battles, on the land as on the sea. . . ."

"Boys and girls . . . boys and girls!" Mrs. Turner came into the room wearing a look which could only be described as undiluted rapture. "I want you all, each and every one of you all, to know that you did yourselves proud. That was about the finest graduation that any school has ever had. Congratulations and I'm sure that you'll all do just fine in the life ahead."

Mrs. Turner further advised us to take "a breather" for the next ten minutes or so or at least until the auditorium chairs were taken off the floor and the sweet table brought on.

I felt inside the pocket of my graduate's gown for my lipstick and pocket comb and then went to the only place in the gym where they have a mirror. The girls' toilet.

Just as I had feared, the place smelled of unflushed urine and just as I feared, I began backing out the door. "Oh, come on," I encouraged myself, "the smell of a little pee isn't going to kill me." I held my breath as I went on with my personal beautification. Finally when I had to come up for air, I told myself not to worry about it because a lot more lethal than this odor is my mother commenting for the whole world's edification on some variation of the theme: How can Patricia go around looking the way she does? And then followed by the inevitable conclusion: Because she's a born slob who doesn't care how she looks. Only the last half of that is a lie. Because, you see, Mother, I do care. I do very much care.

The gym was now cleared of its folding chairs and in its place were dozens of people clusters. Many of the clusters had a black-garbed graduate as a nucleus. The very largest cluster, though, had our pink-cheeked state representative at its core.

And there on the opposite side of the cookie and punch table was my very own cluster of five. I felt vaguely embarrassed about my grandparents. They looked too prosperous, too non-Protestant, and far too citified for this poor, rural bible-belt community. I guess my own parents once seemed that way too, but after twenty years of running the biggest store in Jenkinsville surely everybody is very used to them, by now.

At my cluster's hub, not surprisingly, was Mother, whose carefully preserved beauty struck me afresh. Only a few times—on a few rare moments—have I actually been able to translate her obviously admirable features and lovely figure into beauty. But because just about everybody else automatically makes the translation, I know that it has to exist, only not for me. Not at all for me.

Maybe I'll give her an honest compliment. Tell her how beautiful she looks. Well, why not! Aren't graduations a time to put away old things? To try for new beginnings?

When my grandpa saw me approach, he broke out into a little run to greet me with a full wraparound hug. "*Mazeltov,* my darling Patricia! Hmmm . . . such a graduate."

13

Then Grandma placed her freshly lipsticked lips against my cheek and I got to hoping that her pink print wouldn't stain me for the duration of the day.

Without actually making contact, my father made a slight kissing sound next to my cheek. And as I turned to give my mother my compliment, she gave me an obligatory kiss and an obligatory smile before saying, "I see you've combed your hair. Too bad you didn't remember to do that *before* the ceremony."

I must have combed my hair before the procession. I couldn't have forgotten something that important, could I? An image of how horrendous I looked with my hair as unkempt as an orangutan thrust itself upon me. I felt private fury over my public humiliation.

"I was really hoping, Mother"—I heard the sounds of a hurt little girl within my own voice—"that on my graduation day you would have been able to find something nice to say."

"Well, I certainly did," she insisted. "I said your hair sure does look a heck of a lot better now than it did while you were up there on the stage."

I remember asking my mother years ago why was it that she said so many things that hurt my feelings. And I can still see her laughing riotously as though she were enjoying herself for the first time in a long time. "You oughta thank me," she said. " 'Cause I'm the only one who cares enough about you to tell the truth. Are you such a baby, Patricia, that you'd let the truth hurt?"

Maybe those had been the words that had robbed me of my clean, unobstructed right to anger. All I know for sure is that somewhere, someplace, my private fury became mixed and muddled with guilt every time she made me her victim. Was it fair to become angry with her just because I was too much of a baby to handle the truth?

But one question continued to nag at me: Was she actually saying all these debilitating things for my own good? And were her constant reminders about my hair, my clothes, and my general lack of attractiveness actually painful or did it only seem to be so to supersensitive me? Because what wounds me wouldn't necessarily wound anybody else. And certainly wouldn't wound her. Would it?

After all, I can't believe—I mean, why on earth would a person who's supposed to love me stretch so far to maim? Over and over I asked myself if they would. I told myself that they wouldn't. That she wouldn't!

I guess it was Madame Curie, more than anybody else, who showed me what it was I had to do.

Lying across my bed one evening last winter, I was reading a biography of the great scientist which told how she had to laboriously go through eight tons of pitchblende to isolate just one gram of radium.

Well, in some way, it struck me that I had to do that too. Had to scientifically find a way to isolate the essential gram of truth from among Mother's vast volume of words and actions.

If I could devise a kind of replica of one of my mother's insults and then use it against her while at the same time proclaiming that I'm only doing it in the name of love, how would she respond? If she didn't bleed, wouldn't that prove that there was nothing intrinsically wrong or brutal about her and her words? That there is only something off target with me for reacting so vehemently to so little stimulation?

By the time I had perfected my plan for isolating my own gram of reality, several weeks had passed and it was Thursday, December 29. I told myself that it was necessary for me to wait two more days. Mustn't dilute the effect. Must wait until she was most vulnerable—until New Year's Eve.

She was wearing a silver lamé evening dress which hugged the generous, but still surprisingly solid, curves of her thirty-eight-year-old body. And even without the upper swell of her breasts, she would have received attention. Had to give her credit for that.

She fluffed her black almost shoulder-length hair away from her ears, while her diamond earrings (borrowed from Grandma) caught the light from the vanity table's lamp. I watched her eyes flutter down and then up as a smile of coy acceptance was being manufactured for her lips. She was already enjoying the masculine attention that she was soon to receive.

I drifted deeper into her bedroom to lean against the edge of her pink satin bedspread. "Getting ready for the big dance?" I asked while wondering if I had either the heart or the stomach to follow through on the plan. But I had to. Had to end the confusion and the guilt. Once and for all, I had to know if I had the right to my own anger.

"If I talk to you, you'll make me late."

I tried for my pleasant voice. "What time does it start?"

"No special time."

"Don't you have to meet the others at the Peabody Hotel at a certain time?"

"If we leave Jenkinsville by five thirty, we should be in Memphis by six thirty, and I wish you'd stop gawking and let me get dressed."

"Sorry, didn't mean to gawk. It was just . . . just your hair," I said, wondering if I had left enough bait.

Slowly she made a forty-five-degree turn. "What about my hair?"

Without answering, I rose to appraise my mother's hair. She was waiting for me, for my judgment, and it made me feel powerful. "It's nothing," I shrugged. "Nothing important."

"What do you mean by that?"

"I only meant that I don't want to upset you . . . not on your big night."

"Tell me what's WRONG!"

I heard myself sigh like she sighs. As long as I could remember it was one of mother's short-cut ways of telling me that I was wasting far too much of her valuable time. "Well, it was just that I was wondering why you didn't ask Eileen to put a rinse in your hair. All of those gray roots are beginning to show."

"That's NOT true. You're imagining things!" Her voice was pitched up an octave. "You know that I would never let my roots show!"

"Patty darling," said my grandma in an uncommonly fast flow of words. "Now that school's out maybe you'll come to Memphis. Visit with Grandpapa and me."

"Well . . ." I said, waiting to see whether or not she was going to include Sharon in the invitation. It's not that I dislike my fourteen-year-old sister, although God help me, sometimes I do. It's just that I'm tired of being compared to Sharon the pretty or Sharon the sweet. But more than that I hate Sharon for depriving me of my alibis.

One of my really comforting alibis states that people would like me if only I were a Baptist. Well, Sharon is no more Baptist than me and everybody likes her. And then there's the most comforting alibi of them all: My parents don't know how to love anybody, so why be disappointed that they don't love me? The only problem with that is that they do like her pretty well.

But it's okay, Sharon, I can understand that. Most of the time (if we can forget those few ugly times when my jealousy flared) I like you too. A whole lot.

The really strange thing about my grandparents is that in spite of Sharon's obviously superior virtues, they—I must be mistaken—but they do seem to love me more.

Grandpa mentioned that I could have "almost full use" of the Buick while Grandma talked on about the Ridgeway Country Club. "The pool is open and I think it's past time you started mingling with some of your own."

She turned to her daughter. "Pearl, if you don't want Patty to marry some *goy,* then you have to see to it that she mixes and mingles with her own kind. Being the only Jew in town is no good!"

It was then that Edna Louise Jackson's mother poked her head into our cluster. "Forgive me for intruding, Pearl, but what did you and Harry think of Edna Louise's speech? Just forget that I'm her mother and tell me what it is you truly . . . believe."

"Why, Cora," said my mother, "now nobody in this world has to tell you that Edna Louise always does a fine job at whatever it is she does."

Mrs. J. G. Jackson trilled a laugh. "Oh, now, I wouldn't say 'always.' "

"Well, I would," insisted my mother. "And not only that, she's the most outstanding person for a girl that I've ever met."

My father added, "Not only did she give a fine speech, but she sure did look pretty as a picture."

What I wanted to do was scream at my parents. Scream out that Edna Louise wasn't their daughter. *I* was, and I needed something too! But instead of screaming, I dug my nails so deep into my palms that I felt stinging, and then I squeezed out a smile so that neither of them would ever suspect that I so much as cared.

Edna Louise Jackson's mother lit up like a five-hundred-dollar juke box. "Oh, I thought she looked right nice too. And her words were inspiring, weren't they, Harry? Truly inspiring."

Then my mother suddenly remembered to introduce Mrs. Jackson to "my parents, the Frieds, from Memphis." After a round of pleasantries, Mrs. Jackson found her way back to the subject of Edna Louise. It was as though she hadn't been completely nourished by my mother's and father's banquet of compliments and was now attempting to extract another feast from my grandparents. But they both refused to feed her. I guess I knew somehow that they'd give to me before they'd give to a stranger.

Mrs. Turner cruised past our cluster. "Patricia, go line up with the others. Representative Stebbins wants to personally congratulate all the graduates."

I got in line behind Edna Louise (sometimes it seems as though all of Jenkinsville gets in line behind Edna Louise) to await my turn to shake hands with the great man. Superintendent Begley introduced her. "This is one little lady we're all mighty proud of, Miss Edna Louise Jackson. She was not only Class President, but was also voted Most Likely to Succeed."

Representative Stebbins pretended to chuckle. "Well, well, well, looks like I'm going to have some fierce competition from you in the political arena some day."

"You probably know of Edna Louise's daddy," added Mr. Begley.

Mr. Stebbins's face was caught in a moment of surprise. "Jackson? Now don't you go telling that your daddy is Mister J. G. Jackson?"

"Why, yes, sir," Edna Louise smiled coyly. "He surely is."

When it came my turn, our superintendent introduced me as "the daughter of one of Jenkinsville's leading merchants, Patty Bergen."

"Patty Bergen," repeated Mr. Stebbins as though he was trying to make a connection. "Where have I heard that name before? Weren't you one of our fine Stebbins-for-Representative workers last year?"

"Uh, no, sir," I answered, trying to get distance between us before the connection was made. But by the time I had reached the gym's outer limits, I had already begun my medicinal self-ridicule: The only search for a connection that was going on was in my own imagination. An important man—a lawmaker like Representative Billy Bruce Stebbins—would have more pressing things on his mind than attempting to conjure up some long-forgotten newspaper stories of six years ago.

As a great sense of relief and foolishness swept over me, I turned suddenly to glance back at our commencement speaker, who was caught—caught staring at me as Mr. Begley, cupping his hand around his mouth, spoke directly into the legislator's ear.

I felt fury freeze my face. I'll never speak your name again. You, Mr. Begley, are the worst. Always pretending to like me, pretending that I'm as good as anybody else. Well, I'm not as good as anybody else! Even before Anton, not you or anybody else hereabouts would ever believe that a Jewish girl could be as good as anybody else.

Then my internal thermostat whose job it is to keep everything temperature-controlled at 98.6 must have experienced a sudden collapse. Fever, like a windwhipped fire, began raging through my body and up toward my brain. I was afraid that I was going to burn to death.

As I reached the oversized gym door, I tried to push. Wanted to get to the air and away from the people. Wanted to push, but I couldn't. Couldn't do anything, but hold onto the wooden door brace. Had to hold on just to keep from going down.

Someone—it was a woman—asked me if I was fainting and as I watched the gym spin and blacken, I answered, "No." Then Mrs. Turner materialized to ask me a variation of the same question. This time I closed my eyes against all questions while making sickness my only concern.

"She's burning up!"

"Her folks are over there."

"Get them!"

The thought of either my mother or father rushing to my aid, placing their hands on my forehead, supporting my weakness with their bodies, helped me gather what strength I had left. Using it all against the cumbersome door, I opened it and half tumbled out into the dank day.

The outside wall of the gym steadied me as I groped my way around the whitewashed building. Directly in back, I stopped in front of a clump of unkempt grass. My head was revolving clockwise while my stomach was heading counter-clockwise.

"ULP!" I watched with uncommon interest as the green clump took on a sour-smelling, lumpy, cream-colored covering and I knew that I was already recovering, for my mind briefly strayed to things other than my state of health. I began to suspect, for example, that I'd never again eat chicken à la king and, for the first time, it occurred to me to be grateful that I had been a bottle baby. For if my sour-spirited mother had nursed me, it could have only been with clabbered milk.

At the outside bubbler, I swished water around my mouth, vigorously patted my face with wet hands, combed my hair, put on fresh lipstick, and came to the conclusion that chances were excellent I'd recover. There was only a little weakness left and anybody can tell you that that just isn't in the same league with burning queasiness of the stomach.

Anyway, I think I'm okay now and maybe I should be grateful to the behind-my-back whisperings of Coach Begley for teaching me something that I had never really wanted to learn: Once a penalty is called against a player it is in effect for the duration of the game.

Just because it's been a good long while since anybody has called me "Natz" or "Nazi lover" doesn't mean that people have suddenly stopped remembering. Because every once in a while, I catch a certain look—a certain strange uncomprehending look—on somebody's face and I know, know as sure as anything, that they're thinking about me and what I did for a German prisoner-of-war so long ago.

As I re-entered the gymnasium, I saw the back of a familiar well-tailored, glen-plaid suit. My father was speaking to Mrs. Turner. "You're not making sense. If she fainted then where is she?"

I smiled what I hoped would pass for a sincere smile. "Hi, how are you all enjoying the party?"

"Mrs. Turner just told me you fainted," said my father, who sounded for the first time since coming here as though he was no longer bored.

"Sir?" I asked, while trying to face-register surprise as I wondered just why it is that I'd go through almost any kind of deception, at almost any price, to keep my parents from ever seeing me weak and needy. Physically or emotionally. It was all the same.

"What I said," corrected Mrs. Turner, "was that Patty lost every speck of color as she held onto that door for dear life."

"I did get a little warm," I admitted cheerfully, "under this old black gown, so I went out to the bubbler for a drink."

My mother was quickly approaching, but from fifteen or twenty feet away, she called out, "Did you really faint?"

Some five or six people nearby, including Mr. Casper Willis and his spinster daughter, Rachel, who had been unaware of the incident, turned to gape at me. Probably they were very annoyed to have missed out on the greatest drama since that Sunday morning Reverend Benn preached from the pulpit with a freshly blackened eye.

Maybe they're thinking that if I truly cared about their amusement, I'd stage something really interesting. Perhaps

23

the ancient and honorable Japanese ritual of disembowelment or, at the very least, an epileptic seizure, preferably grand mal.

Within reaching out and touching distance, my mother came to an abrupt halt. "Well, what's wrong with you?"

"I got so hot wearing this old black gown that I had to go outside to the bubbler for a drink."

She looked at me suspiciously as though some valuable tidbit was being withheld from her. "Tell the truth, you were sick to your stomach again, now weren't you?"

"I already told you."

"This is the third time lately. Somebody must have said *boo* to you," she said loudly enough to satisfy Rachel Willis's ongoing interest in Mother's observations.

"Nobody said *boo* to me, honest."

"Well, somebody must have," she insisted. "Because every time someone says *boo* to you, you vomit."

· 3 ·

AT TEN MINUTES AFTER FOUR (exactly one hundred thirty minutes after the start of the graduation ceremonies) all six of us crowded into my father's sun-baked Chevy. When he zoomed on down Highway 64, neglecting to take the first right turn which would have taken us through the two business and the two residential blocks which comprise Jenkinsville, Arkansas (population 1,170), I knew that he wanted to cool off his car.

On the other side of Bud's Gulf station, my father tapped on the right-hand side of his windshield. "Look over there, Sam. That red brick house going up."

When Grandpa acknowledged seeing what someday soon was going to be a "nice little house," my father continued, "You're a real estate man, Sam. How many good houses would you guess have been built here in Jenkinsville in the last five years?"

"Oh, not many. Not more than four or five a year since the end of the war. Twenty, twenty-five, say thirty houses in all."

"I'll tell you better'n that," said my father. "That's only the second house of any kind that's been built here since the war. This town is stagnating!"

"Lots of up-north industries, Harry, are looking for quiet places with cheap labor. First thing you have to do is band together with the other merchants."

My father made a hissing sound. "I'd sooner band together with a bunch of rattlesnakes. Once we had us the Jenkinsville Mercantile Association. It was back during the war when everybody was making a buck. There was six of us leading merchants who (thanks to me) were real successful in getting people for miles around to come into town on a weekday. We handed out free tickets every Wednesday, every time anybody made a purchase.

"And at exactly eight o'clock on Wednesday night, there'd be a drawing in front of the picture show and that's when the grand prize of fifteen dollars was handed out. Well, Jesus H. Christ, you never saw so many people crowding into one small town in your life. From as far away as

Cherry Valley they chugged into town in old trucks and battered cars that cranked from the front."

"And I'll never for the life of me forget," added my mother, "the preacher's wife coming into the store fit to be tied, telling us that we were playing Satan's game by luring folks into town on a weekday. 'Why,' she complained in that whiny little voice of hers, 'I couldn't even park my own car in front of my own house. All those niggers and rednecks just a-choking up the streets.' "

"I didn't care about that bitch!" said my father. "It wasn't her. It was the big cotton planter, George C. Henkins, who killed Wednesday. At the dinner meeting of the Rotary Club, he read out a resolution asking the merchants to dispense with Wednesdays. He talked about how it's only patriotic keeping the sharecroppers working in the fields where they belong. Cotton is needed for the war effort. And we all have to make sacrifices in wartime.

"Well, sir, no sooner did George get his speech out than the other five merchants practically wet their pants agreeing.

"But I stood up to him and I mean to tell you that I was the only one to do it. Looking him right in the eye, I told him: 'I want you all to know right here and now that I'm as patriotic as the next man. And maybe more so! But I'd like George to answer me, why in God's name do I have to ruin my business to see that your fields get picked? More money in your pockets!'

"Well, old George lifted his hands for quiet just like he was fixing to sermonize. 'Now, Harry, I'm surprised to hear you say that, really I am.' He was talking softly as if to say that he didn't know cotton prices was going straight through the roof. " 'Cause I thought you, of all people, appreciated what this war is all about. We Americans, trying to save *your* people from the Nazis.' "

When my father turned off Highway 64 at the First Baptist Church of Jenkinsville corner, I knew that the car, if not the passengers, was considered sufficiently cooled.

We cruised down Main Street past the Rice County Bank, the post office, the picture show where the marquee announced Deborah Kerr and Stewart Granger in *King Solomon's Mines.*

In front of the largest store in town, the car rolled to a stop. Because I sensed that some sort of recognition was needed by my father, I found myself reading aloud the big, bold, black sign that was touched for emphasis with a dash of red. "Bergen's Department Store," I sang out like a radio announcer thrilled by the opportunity to deliver a hard sell. "Quality Goods for the Whole Family. Shoes, clothing, hardware, and variety."

After my recitation, my father drove back to our six-room white frame house with the screened-in side porch. We all lunched on the lean corned beef, kosher dills, potato salad, and fresh pumpernickel that my grandparents had brought all the way from Rosen's Delicatessen in Memphis.

And shortly after that Grandma reached into Grandpa's inside suitcoat pocket to bring out a long white envelope for me with the printed return address:

S. Fried & Sons, Realty Co.
240 N. Main St.
Memphis, Tenn.

As I took the envelope, I noticed that both of them were smiling proud smiles. Why are they doing that? If I was something to be proud of, wouldn't my own parents know that too? Wouldn't they be the first to see it? Maybe, no credit to me, grandparents are practically genetically compelled to love their grandchildren. What else could it be?

Still I don't understand them. They were about the only people who always acted as though I had nothing in this world to be ashamed of. When people from all over this country exploded over the fact that a Jewish girl would actually hide an escaped German prisoner, my grandparents considered it not much more than a *mishegoss*.

I wish that word was in my big Webster's International Dictionary because I'd like to know precisely what it means. But I'm pretty sure that it means making a fuss over nonsense. Like when my mother cries to Grandma about some slight from Uncle Irv, then Grandma usually says something like: "Pearl, you're being silly. It's all a *mishegoss*."

At any rate, my grandparents were convinced that my being sent to reform school was more of a disgrace for the people of Arkansas than it was for me. "Nothing but a bunch of rednecked anti-Semites! Since when does a human person have to get credentials before they're allowed to give food to a hungry man?"

Actually, I wasn't as innocent as that. Because all the time I was hiding Anton in those abandoned rooms above our garage, I knew I might get into trouble, but I also knew that it wasn't wrong. Not what God would consider wrong! Wish I could just once talk to somebody . . . almost anybody! I'd like to explain it to them. I'd want them all to understand that Anton didn't escape our prisoner-of-war camp to bomb our cities or even to return to Germany to fight again.

Only thing in this world that he wanted was to be a free man. Why is that so impossible to believe? But I'd have no more luck getting people to believe that than I would getting them to believe something else which is equally true. Outside of Ruth, Frederick Anton Reiker was the finest person that I've ever known.

"Well, aren't you going to open it?" asked Grandpa, who had, in fact, taken the envelope from me to remove the handwritten card inside. "I wrote it, so I'll read it." He adjusted his glasses and cleared his throat. "Poetry it's not."

"Just read," said Grandma. "And leave the commenting to Walter Winchell."

"A-hem. It says: To Patty our dearly beloved granddaughter on her graduation day, we give this check so that it can help you prepare for your life and your work at the college whichever you choose. Love and kisses from Grandma and Grandpa."

I ran into Grandpa's arms so that nobody would even suspect my tears. Part of it was that they could still love me in spite of everything. And the other part was the awful suspicion that they'll stop loving me once their gift money is spent on something other than college. It won't be spent on anything but college! I can still stop myself! I am very much in control.

Because if I did spend my money on that, then they, like me, would consider it nothing but a betrayal. A bare-faced betrayal.

"Now that you've heard the sentiments from the heart,"

said Grandma, adjusting a diamond stud in her ear, "you aren't a tiny bit curious to see how much the check is for?"

I nodded yes while wondering if they had forgotten telling me periodically over the last few years about their plan to give me a thousand dollars for each year that I stay in college.

Grandma patted my shoulder. "It's for a thousand dollars."

It took several swallows to clear my throat of enough tears to be able to express just how much I appreciated both them . . . and their check.

Later when my mother, Sharon, and I (my father was napping) walked my grandparents out front to their well-polished black Buick, Grandma said, "Patty, darling, take the morning train to Memphis next Wednesday. Stay for at least a week. We'll buy college clothes."

I searched for the words to tell her, to tell them both, that I didn't know if I'd be needing college clothes. That everybody had been operating under certain false assumptions which I had more or less deliberately perpetuated.

But then if I said that, wouldn't Grandpa ask, "What false assumptions?"

Well, I wouldn't have to answer much more than I don't think I'll go to Memphis State College or even the University of Alabama this fall.

Grandma might add that there are other places where Jewish boys and girls meet. Places like the University of Texas. And so where did I plan to go?

What could I say then? How could I even begin to explain something to them that I have never satisfactorily been able to explain to myself? Even the first part of it, the going-to-Europe part, would be incomprehensible to them. Grandfather would raise his voice: Jews don't go *to* Europe. They come *from* Europe.

I understand that, I tell him as I feel my dream begin to sink beneath the moving sands of never-never land.

Probably my grandmother would start remembering again, would start crying, "My sisters Toby and Miera, their husbands and children, they'd all be alive today if they had only left Europe in time. . . ."

And I couldn't argue with them because they're not what you'd call wrong. Not wrong at all. But they're being right doesn't help me. Doesn't help me with the obsession!

Grandpa helped Grandma into the front seat and after some last minute hugs, kisses, and farewell waves, the Buick headed off in the direction of Highway 64.

Still waving, Sharon said, "They're real nice." Her words seemed to be invested with meaning beyond their meaning.

Automatically I dropped my arm around her shoulder. "That's for sure," I answered, wondering if my own words came out equally invested.

Because I needed to be alone and Sharon obviously needed company, it took me a good half hour before I was able to slip away. I walked into our garage which is located halfway between our house and the railroad tracks and looked up at the non-existent stair boards which my father (with his characteristic attention to detail) had removed twelve years ago when he bought this property. Said he wanted to keep hoboes from finding a home in our abandoned over-the-garage servants' quarters.

I successfully balanced myself step by careful step on the thick brace boards to climb to the place which I even now

32

think of as "Anton's hideout." Propping myself back against the desk that I had so many years ago fashioned from forgotten sawhorses and a discarded door, I tried "seeing" him.

Sometimes it's so hard to do. Oh, I can still describe just how and where his hair fell across his forehead and exactly where in his hazel eyes those specks of green were located. And even now, I can still remember how his lips felt when they kissed me goodbye. Then why can't I bring him back whenever I want . . . whenever I need to?

Once I even went so far as to position my nails on my cheeks. See Anton, I threatened myself, or take the consequences! When no matter how hard I tried, I still could not bring him back, I screamed, "Last chance!" But still no images came, so without any more warning, both nails plowed beneath the skin's white surface to open a ragged row of red.

I guess it was that experience of pain self-inflicted which, more than anything else, taught me that there are still some things that not even violence can effect.

What I have learned is that I can find Anton just at those times when I'm least needy, least demanding. Last Monday —it might have been Tuesday—I rode my bike a couple of miles up Highway 64 until I reached the secluded banks of the St. Francis River. As I settled down among the knee-high river grasses with a single bent Lucky Strike stolen from my father's pack, it came to me that if only I closed my eyes, he would be there waiting for me. And I saw him too. Exactly as he was during that summer.

With my eyes still closed, I spoke to the vision that was sealed somewhere between my pupils and my lids. "I'm

33

happy to see you again." But when he didn't respond to my greeting, I went on. "I think I've told you all this before, Anton, but in some ways your death is still very fresh to me."

When something funny happens, like when Jimmy Wells gave us his impression of one of Coach Begley's pep talks and I'll be right in the middle of a laughing jag and then it'll hit me . . . hit me hard. Anton is dead and I am alone so why am I laughing? Why in the world am I laughing?

Sometimes I ask myself, knowing as I do that the only way to avoid the pain is to have never met you, would I choose that? But what I get is not so much an answer as a remembering. Like the first time I saw you. You had come into my father's store with a bunch of prisoners-of-war. And everybody (even the guards) wanted field hats, but not you, Anton. Why was that? They made you chop cotton too, didn't they? Was it because you knew you wouldn't be hanging around those fields very long? Or was it because field hats weren't your style? Just another symbol of your servitude.

The next time I saw you was just minutes after the escape. You were running along the railroad embankment. Even from the distance of the room above our garage, I knew that it had to be you and I also knew that I'd never allow the 5:15 to take you away.

But it wasn't until you stopped running, to hide yourself against the railroad embankment, that I caught up with you. I called your name; you turned in terror. I told you it was okay; it was only me. Only Patty. But what I was thinking was that you don't ever have to be afraid again because I don't ever intend to let anything bad happen to you. Not ever!

I took you to a safe place, too, because ever since the stair boards were ripped off, nobody else had ever been up here.

Right off, I thought you were the smartest person that I've ever known and so I asked you to teach me to be smart too. And you know what you said? Without so much as a hesitation or a phony emphasis, you said, "You already are." And I began to believe that too.

You see, not in school or anywhere else could I do anything well, so naturally enough people thought me dumb, and yet—and I wouldn't tell this to anybody but you—sometimes I think I know what people are meaning even when they're a long way from saying what it is they're meaning.

And other times, I even think I know what people are feeling even when they're doing their best to hide just what it is they're feeling. Right away you noticed that about me. You were the only person to have ever noticed that about me. I was so thrilled that I can still hear your words. "You have," you said while pantomiming an aerial over your own head, "an incredible set of antennae."

So I guess the fact that outside of Ruth you were the first person to ever treat me as though I had value was the first thing that I liked about you. But there was more. Oh, there was so much more!

There was your face. That was one thing that I loved about you. I considered it the very face that God would use should He ever decide to make an earthly visit. And did you know that it revealed as much—more sometimes—than even your words. But don't go thinking that your words were just Arkansas-ordinary 'cause they weren't! Sometimes they made me laugh and lots of times they made me think. And I even remember one time when they made me cry.

That was the night that you left the hideout for the last time. Through the darkness, I led you to the spot where the trains always slow down before taking on the big curve. Well, somewhere en route, you asked me if you were still my teacher.

I must have answered yes. At any rate, I'm not vague about what came next. That's when you said, "Then I want you to learn this, our last lesson. Even if you forget everything else I want you to always remember that you are a person of value."

Then with a dignity that bordered on ceremony, you placed your ring on my finger and added, "And I want you never to forget that you had a friend who loved you enough to give you his most valued possession."

I cried because this was the most beautiful moment I had ever known and I cried because the loneliness that I was soon to know was going to have more reality than any I had ever known before.

And, Anton, it's still a struggle trying to see myself through your more loving view of me. Still I try. . . .

There was so much that you made me feel. To this day, I don't know whether there was one feeling that was more important than any other, but there was something that I felt all during those days that we spent together. And I feel it still. Probably you'll think this the ranting of an eighteen-year-old. Just the same, I'm going to tell you: Your friendship honored me. Far beyond anything that has happened to me either before or after, your friendship honored me.

Sometimes I read about somebody being honored for writing a newspaper story: the Pulitzer Prize. Or for stopping a war: the Nobel Prize. And I think the only advantage that their honor has over mine is that they can talk on and on about theirs. While I? I must never even speak of mine.

• 4 •

AT SIX O'CLOCK on Wednesday morning, the alarm clock went off. I wanted plenty of time to bathe, dress, and finish packing without having to rush down to the depot to catch the 8:15 to Memphis.

I walked up Silk Stocking Street, which most folks refer to as Jenkinsville's only residential street without taking into consideration that jelly-roll shaped street where the blacktop ends known to one and all as "Nigger Bottoms." Dragging behind me was my father's heavy brown leather suitcase which had been on so many buying trips to St. Louis that my father says it's perfectly capable of making the trip alone. That's one of his jokes.

I looked overhead into the full face of the morning sun and made myself the promise that I was not going to spend my life in a place where the sun is able to sear away the freshness of morning even before eight.

"Hey, Patty, where you heading with a suitcase this time of the morning?" asked Mrs. Burton Benn, the strict-faced wife of the Baptist minister, who was standing on her front porch with a head that looked as though it was sprouting a fresh crop of bobby pins.

"I'm eloping."

There was a thinking woman's silence before a knowing smile came over Mrs. Benn's face. "Now, you don't mean it."

I laughed. "No, I guess I don't. I'm going to Memphis to visit my grandparents for a week."

"Them's your mother's folks? The ones I met at your graduation last week?"

"That's right."

Miriam Benn waved from the fingers. "Well, you just tell 'em that I said hi."

As I walked up the steep gravelly grade of the station house, more dragging than carrying the increasingly heavy suitcase, I saw her. She was looking down the opposite track so that she couldn't possibly have seen me. Thank God for that! I backed far enough down the grade to stay out of sight. Maybe I could find somebody to drive me the ten miles to Earle; I could pick up the train a few miles farther down the track. What's the bus schedule? Doesn't matter. Grandmother is meeting me at Union Station, not at Trailways.

I looked at my watch. Not yet eight o'clock. Still time to unscramble my brains. I sat on the edge of my suitcase and began unscrambling: Number one, there is absolutely no way that I can reach Memphis's Union Station by 9:35 other than by catching the 8:15 from Jenkinsville.

And number two: Why does an old Negro woman, of all people, scare me so very much?

She doesn't—at least not in the "I'm gonna getcha" sense of that word. Just maybe the problem is that more than anybody else, Ruth understands me. And that scares me! When I was released from the Bolton School, I wanted to show everybody in this town that what I went through was no big deal. I was not one bit beaten down because the reformatory was just another punishment, not all that different from being kept in after school.

So to convince everybody, I became a clown. Whee! I'm having so much fun just a-talking too much and laughing too loudly.

Maybe I convinced them all, but I could never have convinced Ruth. She would have known better.

For it was her body that I threw myself against while crying that she couldn't leave me. "You can't leave me here!" And even though I kept reminding myself that I was very young then, having "celebrated" my thirteenth birthday at Bolton, I still couldn't face up to the raw self-exposure.

Knowing that Ruth can never again see me as being strong, because somewhere during her Bolton visit I admitted to her what I had never before admitted, even to myself. That I needed someone. I needed her. And there's still

40

another phrase that no matter how hard I try, I cannot scrub from my consciousness. Clinging to her as though she were my life raft and I was far from land, I said, "I'm afraid to be without you."

In all my life, nobody had ever seen me so weak and vulnerable. The illusion of my strength had shattered a lot like the Harrisburg levee after the river came crashing through.

I had always believed that if I ever exhibited any weakness then I couldn't survive. Or if I did, I would be treated with all the open contempt that I deserved. That's what I thought up until sometime last winter when I saw what happened to Charlene Madlee in the parking lot of the *Commercial Appeal*.

I had been up to see Mr. Chuck Brennan, the paper's mid-South editor, about an idea that I had for a feature story. And not only did he agree to the idea provided I could get proper documentation, but my old friend Charlene, one of the paper's star reporters, said that she was going to make time from an impossible day to go out for a sandwich with me.

Six years ago, it was the same Mr. Brennan who sent Charlene to Jenkinsville to cover the story of the escaped prisoner-of-war. And later when I became a prisoner, it was Charlene who suggested to Mr. Brennan that maybe I could try to write a story about the "real" conditions inside the Bolton reformatory.

Well, the article with my fancy pen name was released (in all five editions) upon the people of Memphis and the mid-South even before I was. I can still see the headline:

by Antonia Alexander

As Charlene and I crossed the back lot, a large, dark, prosperous-looking car rolled backward, striking her. But since the brakes had been released without the motor being on, she was not so much struck as bumped.

The purple-tinted head of a shocked matronly lady extended out the car window. "Are you all right?"

At that, Charlene went limp. Turning toward me and dropping her head against my shoulder, she answered with a "noooo . . . " which trailed off into a continuum of sobs.

Even so I understood that Charlene's injury was more psychological than physiological. The last emotional trauma of a traumatic day. My first thought was that this extraordinarily capable lady couldn't possibly want comforting from me. Not from someone half a head shorter and a dozen years younger. My second thought was that she did. That by God, she did!

I closed my arms around Charlene, pressing her forearm with my hand to show her that she wasn't alone. Not a bit! And taking care of somebody else made me feel good. Like discovering you're more than you thought you were. More even than you hoped to be.

As Charlene's control began returning, she explained that she was okay. "It's just that every goddamn soul on the city desk is on my back."

I was pleased that Charlene was visibly returning to herself, and I was pleased that I had been able to give her some comfort, but I was still feeling a sadness from an unspecified direction descending upon me.

42

As we continued our walk down busy Union Avenue toward Taylor's Grill, she spoke of the new city editor brought in from Louisville "to tighten up the ship. But hell, does all his tightening have to be accomplished by driving his nails into me?"

I was able to make appropriate comments on my friend's dilemma even though most of my energies were reserved for trying to find my way through my own spiritual confusion. It wasn't until about nine o'clock that evening on a chilly Trailways bus a few miles east of Jenkinsville that I even began to stumble around and about the source of my discontent.

It had something to do with giving something to somebody else. From experiencing the pleasure and the pain of giving something to somebody else that nobody since Ruth had ever given to me.

Ruth. I looked at my watch. Already eight o'clock. The train may already be on this side of Earle. And I still haven't cleared all the emotional debris from my brain.

What I don't understand is why I can so easily accept Charlene's weakness, but not my own. Never my own. I searched myself for long forgotten (however fleeting) feelings of revulsion upon first seeing Charlene cry, but I didn't find any. Actually, I think the opposite may have been true. Because, more than anything else, it was her tears that made her real to me.

Then if it's a lie that vulnerability is contemptible, I will also have to learn to accept that for myself. If it's okay for Charlene, then it will have to be okay for me too. Now I know something else. Ruth would have never withdrawn ten years of love because of two minutes worth of hysterics at the Bolton reformatory. She would, though, have withdrawn her love for a far more valid reason. I have treated her badly.

More than anyone, it was Ruth who stood by me, and yet for all these six years, I have tried to avoid her. Avoid Ruth. Avoid the only one who saw me weak. Avoid reviving old memories. At all costs—avoid!

And for all this time, I've had to keep open a very wary eye. If she was on one side of the street, I would nonchalantly stroll to the other. Only once, at the post office a couple of years ago, did we come unavoidably face-to-face. And so we both said hello. Hello. Nothing more than hello.

It's not just that she rekindles the pain, although God knows, she sure does do that! I guess I'm afraid that people will see us together and remember that for so many years Ruth had been our housekeeper. Right up until the time the matter erupted which the local people came to refer to as "Patty Bergen's Nazi." And some people even then suspected that nobody was ever able to prove: "That uppity nigra, Ruth, knew all about Patty's hiding of that Nazi."

I remember Ruth's telling me once that all it takes to get a Negro man strung up from a tree is a little suspicion. Thank God, it takes something a little more than that for a Negro woman.

Even my Memphis lawyer in a moment of intense frustration once blurted out that in all his years of experience nobody before me had ever managed to incorporate three such hated elements—a Nazi, a Negro, and a Jew—into a single case.

44

Anyway, I can't stand any more talking, any more re-hashing! All I want is for people to forget me . . . to forget what happened.

Five minutes after eight. I rose from my suitcase perch while sighing as though I had successfully dealt with all those issues abutting the heart without once touching the heart.

And the heart? It wasn't complicated. Not a bit. Because in all ways that really matter, that old Negro woman waiting up there by the side of the tracks is my mother.

I remember once she was so mad at me she could hardly see straight and still she showed how much she cared. Ruth had just gotten through saying, "The living room is no kinda room to be bouncing balls." Well, looking right at her, I decided to give it one final bounce just to prove that I wasn't easily intimidated. It was that "final" bounce that broke my father's reading lamp.

"If I ever catch you telling yore daddy that it was you what broke his lamp," she said, "then I ain't never going to speak to you again. You hear me a-talking to you, girl?"

Later when my parents came home from the store, I over-heard Ruth telling them, "I'm real sorry, folks, but I reckon I just wasn't paying no attention to where I was heading."

But even before that, one of my earliest memories in-volved rubbing Kiwi shoe polish all over my body because I wanted to be like Ruth. I thought that if I were her color, then she'd somehow be my real mother and she'd love me . . . love me even more.

When that didn't work, I tried scraping the brown off her skin with a butter knife. Ruth told me how she laughed

45

until her stomach muscles ached when I told her, "Mommies ought to be white like their children."

Well, maybe this will only go to prove that I haven't progressed an awful lot since I made that statement a dozen or so years ago, 'cause the color thing still bothers me. I'm simply unable or unwilling to cross the color line to claim the only mother I've ever known. Funny thing is, I don't think that anybody in this town would ever believe that it's even remotely possible for somebody white to love somebody who isn't.

And as big a problem as that is, there are still other things which separate us which may be just as big as the color barrier. Things like religion, education, economics, and my ever-present shame that at eighteen, I still haven't outgrown my need for a mother.

Sometimes I wonder if I would have so desperately missed not having a mother if I hadn't once had Ruth. I know I don't actively miss not having a father. Maybe that's because I know at least two girls with pretty nice mothers, but I'm not sure that I know anybody who has a father worth bragging about.

Well, so what if I still want a mother! So did Lottie McEntee right up until her dying days. Nobody knew for sure just how old old Mrs. McEntee was, but everybody figured that she had to be pressing on a hundred. I know for a fact that at least one of her twelve children, Elvira, has been retired from the post office for better than ten years.

Well, a couple of summers ago, I was in the drug store eating a hot fudge sundae when the pharmacist, Mr. Martin Clapp, asked me if I would mind dropping off a prescription for Mrs. McEntee.

Miss Elvira was real appreciative of the favor that I had done her mother and so she practically insisted that I stay long enough for a visit. Well, Miss Elvira talked on and on about the burden (not that she minded it!) of taking care of a very old and sick lady. But it wasn't any of Elvira's words that I found half so memorable as the single word that the almost century-old Lottie McEntee chanted insistently from her sick bed. "Momma . . . momma . . . please help me, momma. . . ."

I looked at my watch again. Almost eight minutes after eight. The train will be coming along in seven minutes and I still have a ticket to buy. I can always buy it from the conductor. Why am I thinking about tickets or conductors? I'm still scrambled, still don't know what to do!

Patty Bergen, you amaze me. You really do! You with your dictionaries and your memberships in the Book-of-the-Month Club AND the Literary Guild. With all that you are nothing, more or less, than a scared rabbit. For Christ's sake, go on and say hello to Ruth. I seriously doubt that she'll bite you.

This time I grabbed my valise and started up that grade as though I had an unalterable destination in mind. And this time she was looking in my direction. "Hi, Ruth," I said, shocked at the ease with which it was spoken. "How you been?" I asked, while coming still closer.

"I've been doing right well, Miss Patty, I thank you kindly. Euuu-whee . . . you done growed into a pretty woman. Always did have the softest, most-seeing eyes in all of Rice County. You been doing okay?"

"I think so. Last week I graduated."

"I knowed that. Saw your name in the *Rice County Ga-*

zette, sure did. But they is wrong when they say that Miss Edna Louise Jackson is the Most Likely to Succeed 'cause she ain't, but you is! Think she could have written up the fire over in Earle for the *Commercial Appeal*? Well, one day one of your stories gonna win a prize. Ruth knows."

I laughed at Ruth's enthusiasm, but primarily I laughed at myself, for only a minute ago I had been so frightened. "You know, Ruth, I sometimes think that we are the only people in this entire town who don't believe that Edna Louise has achieved heavenly perfection."

This time it was Ruth who laughed. "Reckon you and me always did have an eye for that which was real and that which wasn't."

Ruth. Wonderful Ruth. My loving you hasn't been a mistake. You who know so much and without ever having to study dictionaries or library books. And if you were angry about my neglect, surely you'd have shown that by now. But how could a person be avoided for six years and not be angry? It doesn't make sense, not unless . . . not unless you understood.

She had changed, grown gently older since I had last fully looked at her. Before, her hair didn't have those patches of gray, and the series of fine horizontal lines that I remembered are now tracked by deeper vertical lines which crisscross with regularity.

"Hey, are you going into Memphis too?" I asked. "We could sit together. Kind of catch up."

"Oh, no, Miss Patty, I ain't a-going nowhere. My little grandsons are coming visiting from Wynne City. Did you know my son Robert's a preacher now?"

"Oh, that's wonderful, Ruth. That's what you wanted

more than anything. You always said that Robert had enough natural devilment in him to put the fear of the Lord into the devil himself."

She looked enormously pleased. "All these years done come and all these years done gone, and you still remember what it is that old Ruth done said?"

"I guess so," I said, experiencing something of her wonderment.

Then Ruth spoke again, but the insistent screech of the old 8:15 blotted it out. I asked, "What?"

"Nothing more than a passing thought, Miss Patty. I was recollecting that among all them mess of things that I done told you, you done found stuff worth remembering."

As the train was screeching, hissing, and blowing steam while trying with obvious agony to come to a stop, I just nodded because some noise can't be competed with. Then after waiting long enough for the volume of train noises to subside, I told her, "I found things that I just might never forget."

· 5 ·

At exactly 9:55, the 8:15 from Jenkinsville pulled into the multitracked Union Station. And since the combination passenger and freight train was twenty minutes late and Grandmother wasn't, I spotted her right off in her ripened-cranberry-colored linen suit.

"Patricia darling," she called, before throwing her arms around me in prelude to a kiss, "your grandfather made me promise. First thing, I have to bring you by the office. Oy, does he want to show you off."

She noticed my suitcase, which I had begun to half lug, half drag along. "I'll get a porter," she offered.

"No, thanks. I'm very used to it."

She pointed down the track as though she didn't hear me. "There's one!"

I lifted the suitcase as high off the station platform as I could while straining to capacity muscles that I didn't even know I possessed. "See, it's not the least bit heavy."

Grandmother looked at me as if to say, if you plan to make this a test of wills, then be prepared to lose. But what she actually said was, "It's too heavy for you. You might break something. Maybe an arm."

At Grandmother's beckoning, a Negro redcap came to take the heavy case from my hand. I sighed, partly out of physical relief and partly out of anger. When we reached the car, we waged another battle over just whose quarter the porter should take, and again I lost.

"Grandmother likes to pay for you," she said, starting up the Buick.

I sat next to her, saying nothing, but feeling small, ineffectual, and cheated. Cheated? Well, maybe in a way because for a lousy quarter she had begun moving in on something that didn't belong to her. My life.

I know that sometimes little things bother me that my sister or even my mother wouldn't bother to think twice about. My mother, for example, wouldn't dream of ever picking up anything heavy, and every time she's in Memphis she takes it for granted that Grandmother will pay.

Part of it is that I never like putting people to trouble on my account. Never like having money spent on me. I don't think—I'm not sure I'm worth it.

51

A few blocks down on North Main, Grandmother found a metered space catercorner from the office. The carefully lettered sign on the street-level window read:

S. FRIED & SONS
Commercial * Industrial
Sales Leases * Management
Appraisals * Mortgages
* Insurance *

As I pushed open the glass and brass door, Grandmother pressed the back of my hand. "We're so happy you're here."

I believe she meant it. "And I'm so glad you invited me here," I answered, beginning to believe that I meant it.

Walking past a dozen or so scarred flat-top desks made untidy by somewhat official-looking forms which overflowed from wire baskets, Grandma greeted everyone by name.

My grandpa's corner office had a cluttered, no-nonsense look about it with the single possible exception of a gallery of family pictures that he displayed beneath the clear plate glass which covered the top of his mahogany desk. When we came in, he was on the phone, but he threw us a long-distance kiss while motioning us toward two moderately comfortable-looking green chairs.

He went on talking into the receiver. "Julius, Julius, my friend, listen to me. . . . Will you listen! If you paid a penny less for that site, your own children will call you a *ganef*. What? I'm not going to listen to you, Julius, tell me one more time that the Union Avenue location is too far out. You're about to make an old man *brech*. For your information, this is already nineteen-fifty and downtown Memphis is in *gonzeh tseuris*."

Apparently Julius didn't want to make my grandfather throw up or else Julius became a victim of his persuasion, because only a minute later Grandfather was congratulating him on his foresight. As the conversation began to wind down, Grandpa suddenly asked, "Julius, did I ever tell you about my granddaughter? Only eighteen years old and already a writer. . . . Sure, she gets paid for it! The *Commercial Appeal* . . . She's one of their most regular Arkansas correspondents!"

I beamed inside where it doesn't show. Even though "correspondent" sounded too close to "foreign correspondent" (Marguerite Higgins, Ernie Pyle, et al.) for me to be entirely comfortable with the word. Anyway, outside of my Earle fire story, most of what I send in are only local or county-wide events and those stories run only in the newspaper's Arkansas edition.

Besides, most people think that when you get a byline (which I did only once—yep, the Earle fire story) that the newspaper gives you a lot of money. Well, they don't! For "stringers" like me the pay is a consistent fifteen cents per column inch and a byline doesn't count for anything. At least not monetarily.

As soon as Grandpa hung up, he began introducing me around the office just as if I had won the Pulitzer Prize. I felt vaguely embarrassed. Was Grandpa making a fool of himself . . . of us both? Were they thinking that he should stick with singing the praises of Union Avenue sites because every person in this office had already heard all about their boss's black sheep granddaughter?

When Grandma and I reseated ourselves inside the Buick, she asked me where I would like to go for lunch. I thought about The Krystal, where you can get coffee in a large white mug for a nickel and an exceedingly small round hamburger on a square bun for only twelve cents.

After I thought about The Krystal, I thought about Grandma with her genuine diamond-in-the-ear earrings and the pearls at her neck which are simulated nothing. They are real pearls from real irritated oysters. And when I thought about all of that, I knew I shouldn't think about The Krystal.

It's not that I especially love eating in hamburger joints, it's just that I don't feel quite right about her spending a wad of money on some expensive lunch for me.

Once though when I tried to save her money, she laughed, called me, "cheapskate." And then she asked me why I was forever trying to save her money. My answer was one of those surprise answers—I mean, surprising to me. "I'm not trying to save you money, Grandmother," I told her. "I'm only trying to prevent you from spending it on me."

This time, though, I decided that as long as she insists on taking me out in a, as we say in Jenkinsville, high-on-the-hog way, then I might as well choose the hog. "Well, if it's all right with you," I told her, "I'd really love to return to the place you took me a long time ago. The Skyway on top of the Hotel Peabody. They still have live music there, don't they?"

As the tuxedo-suited maître d' showed us to our table, Bobby Lawrence and his music men were playing "I'll Get By." The maître d' seated us next to what The Skyway is famous for—a circular wall of glass and if you can't quite see the whole world from here, you can, at the very least, see our part of the world. Front Street, Mud Island, the Mississippi River, and, on the opposite bank—tah-dah—Arkansas, "Land of Opportunity," or so every one of our license plates proclaims.

After the waiter had taken our orders, Grandmother settled back into her seat and looked me over carefully before announcing, "Now, Patricia darling, we can talk."

"I guess we can," I answered, thinking how I never fail to give awkward-sounding answers to what I perceive as tension-provoking statements.

"Well," she said, still smiling.

But because I couldn't think of a single thing to add to her smile except, perhaps, one of my own, I settled for returning it.

"Well . . . " she repeated, "so, my darling, you decided yet on a college for the fall?"

I wanted to avoid saying anything that Grandma might later look back on as a lie. "I haven't . . . haven't as yet chosen one," I said, while staring down at the incredible whiteness of The Skyway's linens.

"Remember September isn't far away, darling. But don't worry, 'cause you have plenty of time."

I laughed at her inconsistency, but I think Grandma, who began laughing too, was only responding to my pleasure. Her laughter, like her inconsistencies, made her seem young. I began to wonder if it might not be possible to tell her something about my plans, after all. Maybe she really could understand. And I needed somebody in this world to understand. And if I did find somebody who could, I'd ask them please . . . please explain it to me.

Why can't I just go on to college like everybody else? Certainly, I'm not going to follow through on this other wild and impossible thing? Somewhere along the line I'm pretty sure I'll stop myself.

Grandma began telling me about the Rhapsody-in-Blue dinner-dance next Saturday night at the Ridgeway Country Club. Then she paused a long pause before saying, "Your Aunt Dorothy found you a blind date. He's the son of one of her friends, Estelle Lubin. What's the *boychik*'s name?" Grandma asked just as though he were one of my old friends.

"I never met him."

"Well, you will, darling. His name is Lubin. Marshall Lubin. A very nice boy." She went on talking about Marshall being a college boy from the University of Alabama.

It was then that the formally attired waiter brought Grandma's "seafood supreme" and my shrimp cocktail— ninety-five cents for only six bored shrimps lounging on a bowl of cracked ice!

She told me that she'd like to buy me a new dress for the country club dance. Then she looked at me and sighed. "I want you should have a good time at the party."

That was sure true enough. Grandma always wanted me to have a good time, but I'm not completely comfortable with that either. Did she want me to only because I'm eighteen and that's natural enough, or was it because—is it that she still feels sorry for me?

I remember the first Sunday after I was released from Bolton and we all drove to Memphis to see Grandma. Rushing past my mother and even Sharon, she grabbed me with a strength that I'd never have guessed that she possessed. Then with a startling kind of abruptness, she released my arm to go dashing toward the kitchen. "Something's burning" is what she had said, but the funny thing is I never smelled a thing.

Later, on the ride back to Jenkinsville, I thought a lot about her behavior. Finally it came to me that she must have suffered much more than embarrassment over my stay at the Bolton reformatory. I felt angry with her for trying to shield me from her suffering. Didn't she realize that I could have helped her? Showed her that being there may have been a little bad, but it wasn't all that terrible, for goodness' sake!

But mainly I was angry with her because for all that time (and maybe that was the only really terrible thing) I didn't know that anybody outside of Ruth really cared about my pain. Grandmother's suffering would have shown me that she did.

But she's like everybody else that way. More comfortable in expressing her anger than in exposing her sorrow. Once, I remember, she flared up at Grandpa and he said, "That's a temper you have there." And I caught her smiling as though she were still a young girl and Sammy Fried were nothing but a boy.

She adjusted the silk poet's bow at her neck. "Maybe Estelle's son . . . uh . . . "

"Marshall," I supplied.

"Yes, Marshall," continued Grandma, "could tell you all about the University of Alabama. Lots of the Jewish boys and girls from Memphis go there," she said.

"You know, Grandma, I don't think I would want to go

57

there because . . . " I want to go so far away from the South. Far enough away so that nobody has ever heard my name. ". . . because Alabama is too much like Arkansas. I'd like to try something else. Maybe New York. Maybe Boston."

She smiled, but it was more out of nervousness than pleasure. "So far away?"

"Well, that's okay," I answered, trying to set her mind at ease. "I don't want to go to college anyway." Suddenly I felt as though I had backed away from a lizard into the carnivorous jaws of a crocodile.

Grandma blinked as though she were struck between the eyes. "Don't want to go to college? Get an education. Meet—"

"It's not that I don't want to go!" When am I going to learn to keep my mouth shut? Good Lord, I can't trust myself with anything!

"Then you do want to go?"

"Well . . . I do maybe want to go some day, but I don't want to go yet."

"Sooo and why not?"

"Because I think . . . it's possible that I might have other plans."

"Oh . . . " Grandma made the *oh* sound all round and all inclusive. "Such as what?" And then she peered over the table to take in an unobstructed view of my midsection. Damn! She thinks just like them. Just like my father and mother! Me, who at eighteen would have more experience filling in for one of those vestal virgins than I would for Edna Louise Jackson in the back seat of Herbie Dickinson's Chrysler.

"Grandmother." I called her name with the same degree of firmness that teachers sometimes use with obnoxious students. "What I am thinking about is traveling. Seeing Europe. Stuff like that."

"Europe?"

"Well, yes, maybe."

"Why?"

"Oh, I don't know . . . no particular reason. I guess I've always wanted to travel, see foreign places."

"I've seen them," she said, looking out beyond The Skyway's glass wall. "My whole family has. For so many generations my family lived in Wieliczka. A good word and a helping hand they had for everybody." Grandmother touched her heart. "God is my witness, there was no better family anywhere. But the best of us was Judah! To this day I remember Judah. How handsome he was! Through fifty years, I can still see my brother's face. Time plays no tricks.

"Your grandmother remembers it all. One night a Polish soldier so drunk he couldn't find his way back to his garrison came galloping into Wieliczka. And to the people—our friends and neighbors that we've known all our lives—he tells them to 'find Jews.'

"Find Jews." Grandma gave a faint chuckle. "I cannot stop seeing Judah's face the moment he was beheaded.

"After that my father vowed he'd get our family to a safe place, so giving up the tailor shop, he bribed his way out of Poland and into Luxembourg.

"It wasn't all sunshine there, either, believe me. Poppa went through hard times, we all did until he established his business, but Poppa, *alav hasholom,* was a good tailor and a

59

good businessman. Soon from all over Luxembourg City, the smart people began coming to his shop. *Gott'danken.*

"Later my sisters Toby and Miera both married doctors and I followed young Sammy Fried to America. My sisters and I stayed close over the years. Once or twice a week we wrote; five times they came to America to visit me. Then Hitler, like a plague, marched into Luxembourg, and I never again heard from anyone."

"I know, Grandma, I'm sorry."

Without in any way acknowledging my belated expression of sympathy, Grandma went on talking. "My mother, my sisters, their husbands, eight children, and twelve grandchildren . . . "

"I know," I said again, but this time feeling Grandma's sorrow for our family beginning to re-ignite my hatred for all those who had ever persecuted my people.

She looked directly at me as though she could see things I couldn't. "You don't know! To know is to know that the old countries are bad for the Jews. Poles, Russians, Germans, they're all the same, not caring about right or wrong. Only doing what they're told. And twice as fast when the instructions come from a uniform."

She pointed to the high-school age busboy who wore gold braided epaulets on the shoulders of his red jacket. "If that pimpled boy wearing that fancy jacket would today go to Germany and order the people, God forbid, to find Jews, people would do what they were told. They would find Jews."

"I understand that," I answered, thinking that I would like nothing better than to spend my life personally tracking down all the Nazis that have so far escaped justice.

Grandmother looked at me with a contempt that I had never before seen on her face. "If you understood, you would not go. You are already here, Patty. In the promised land of freedom."

"Grandmother," I said, in a voice chilled by anger. "I'm surprised that I have to remind you of what nobody will ever have to remind me: It wasn't one of your old countries that took away my freedom."

· 6 ·

WITH A TONGUE-DAMPENED index finger, I pressed my eye-lashes back against closed lids. More than once, I had seen Edna Louise do it to a count of one hundred. And you do have to give the devil her due, she really does have curly lashes. She told me that it was an important beauty secret of the movie stars, but I don't know. Somehow, I just can't imagine Ginger Rogers, Lana Turner, or Susan Hayward entering this world with an imperfection.

At the forty-seventh count, the door chimes resounded. "Patty darling, he's here!" said Grandmother, whose sense of expectation equaled my own. "What's-his-name is here!" she said while poking her head into the guest room.

"Marshall Lubin. I know. I heard the chimes." I gave myself a long, inspecting look in the full-length mirror. Grandmother was right. The blue taffeta strapless with the open-toed silver slippers had been a good choice, and I probably looked as good, maybe better, than I had ever looked before. Anyway, I hope he won't be too disappointed.

He was standing, hands in pockets, in the middle of Grandma's vast living room as though on the verge of concluding a brilliant business deal. Marshall Lubin was short, with a broad never-take-no-for-an-answer countenance and when I said, "Hello, Marshall," with a well-practiced smile, he handed me the florist's box that rested beneath his arm.

"Ohh," I said, after removing the cover. "Camellias are my favorite."

"They're gardenias," he said, making those his first in-person words to me.

"They're my favorite, too," I answered quickly, but not too convincingly. "And they smell a whole lot better."

The Ridgeway Country Club was located on a wooded spread at the eastern end of Central Avenue. At the door of the ballroom, a fancy professionally painted sign which rested on an easel announced: The Ridgeway Country Club proudly presents the annual collegiate Rhapsody-in-Blue dinner-dance. Sophisticated music by Ron Rainer.

Our first steps inside the ballroom confirmed what I had feared: Everybody looked so damn belonging . . . so damn

63

elegant out on the dance floor, and where in the world did they learn those fancy steps?

But God bless Ron Rainer, who granted me a reprieve. Pressing his baton between two outstretched palms, he stepped before the standing microphone to announce that dinner was now being served.

Good. That will give Marshall and me a little more time to talk, maybe he'll get to like me a little before he finds out that I never learned to dance.

As he pulled out my chair, I said (Lord, forgive me this lie), "I'm seriously considering going to the University of Alabama. Do you like it there in Tuscaloosa?"

Without exactly answering, he said that his fraternity (ZBT) of which he is treasurer "throws the best parties on campus" and that the University's school of business (of which he is a student—natch!) is "the best in the country."

As I slowly nodded in a way calculated to make him think that I was trying to accommodate myself to the grandeur of it, I instead began wondering whatever happened to the likes of the Wharton School of Finance or Harvard's School of Business? Had they (to keep faith with young Mr. Lubin) dissolved into fantasyland?

But for the first time all evening, Marshall became fascinated with me. (Or was his fascination strictly limited to what he was telling me?) He rubbed his hands together in anticipation for a moment before looking me straight in the eye. "Do you know what's going to be the coming field of the future?"

I was frankly surprised and pleased that he was going to give credit to endeavors other than accounting and I wanted to offer only a well-considered opinion. I thought about aeronautics. More and more people flying farther and faster.

I thought about medical research. And I thought about television. I've read that that newly born industry is on the very brink of conquering illiteracy and spreading culture (bravo Leonard Bernstein!) throughout the land.

Television. It ought to be television, but because Marshall Lubin didn't seem to be the kind of man who could totally endorse a product that couldn't be weighed, sniffed, or reduced to a formula, I looked elsewhere.

To chemicals. Yes, chemicals! I think I got it. Why, scientists are using drugs to cure cancer and depression. "I think that the coming field of the future," I said with all the conviction of a person who's really sure of his or her ground, "is going to be chemicals."

"Chemicals?" Marshall was clearly taken by surprise. "Why did you say that?"

My God, why do I say anything? And why do I spend my whole life outsmarting myself? "I don't know. I just thought—"

"Well, in my opinion," he said, interrupting with all the finesse of the German hordes crossing the Maginot Line, "and in the opinion of people who know, it's got to be accounting."

"Accounting, now that I think about it," I said too quickly to have thought about it. "I think I see your point."

Marshall's face became grave. It was obvious that he had something pretty important to tell me. Outside of being convinced that he wasn't about to propose marriage, I hadn't a clue as to what it might be.

He pointed a stubby finger toward me as though I were one of his disciples. "Accounting," he said, pausing long enough to give the word a kind of solitary significance, "accounting is the field of the future. Consider the acknowledged fact that businesses are getting bigger, more complex. The bigger the business, the more they're going to have to have accountants to protect their corporate structure."

I hate what you do, Marshall. If only I knew you a little better, I'd probably hate you too. Because you have the colossal arrogance to assume that whatever you do, whatever you think, is the best thing worth doing, the best thing worth thinking. My God, Marshall, you must even give your bowel movements reverent consideration!

Anyway, I may be the world's greatest authority on what it is you do. (And I'm not talking about your accounting either.) You see, I've lived for eighteen years under the same roof with Pearl get-yourself-into-every-equation Bergen. My mother is a lot like you, Marshall, in that she can't conceive of being a part of any world whose dead-center focus isn't upon her.

This isn't even mother's most recent example of making herself so shamelessly significant, but for me it's a very memorable example. During the winter months, Alice Sheehan who for fifteen years worked part-time in our store took sick and her husband put her in Memphis's Baptist Hospital where they diagnosed cancer of the liver.

After that my mother would invariably say as she left for one of her weekly excursions into Memphis, "I sure do wish I had time on this trip to visit poor Alice."

Well, during the first week of April, mother still hadn't

gotten around to visiting her so she sent her a one-pound box of Whitman's Sampler, and during the second week of April, "poor Alice" died.

And ever since then I've seen my mother attempt to share top billing with Alice in her final drama. Not once or twice (but I'm pretty sure three times) I heard my mother talk on about that candy. Telling people in a voice laden with emotion, "I'm just so thrilled that I was able to make poor Alice happy in her lifetime."

As I took just the perfect blend of vanilla ice cream and fudge sauce on my spoon, I anticipated the pleasure. So far, this had been the best part of the whole evening. I was finally getting something I wanted and I didn't have to give a thing.

Marshall tapped my shoulder bone. "Want to dance?"

I looked at Marshall's parfait glass. Only a dishrag could've cleaned it better. "Well . . . " I said, automatically standing up as he pulled out my chair. "I just hope that I'm not too tipsy from the wine," knowing somehow that it's more socially acceptable to be clumsy with drink than it is to be clumsy without.

Ron Rainer was playing a slow number. A fox trot. Thank God. Thank Rainer. Marshall faced me with an almost heroic stoicism before taking my hand. It wasn't until then that I realized it was wet with perspiration, but my knees were in even worse shape. I think my bones had begun disintegrating under the sheer weight of my one-hundred-and-eighteen-pound frame.

Yet with all of my suddenly developing symptomatology, I knew there was still one thing that I must never, never do.

So I glued my eyes on Marshall's slightly oversized left ear, all the time telling myself that God would strike me down—POW!—if I should even once look down at my feet.

Then one, two, and three/four . . . We were dancing! One, two, and three/four . . . If there was something simplistic about the way that Marshall viewed accounting as world pivoting, there was something equally simplistic in the way he viewed dancing. One, two, and three/four . . . But I guess I shouldn't complain, it does make it that much easier to follow.

It was pretty near one o'clock when Marshall cut his car's motor in front of my grandparents' home. There was a light shining outside the front door and with no competing noises to interfere, it sounded as though every grasshopper in East Memphis were in concert.

Marshall dropped his arm around my bare shoulder and lugged me over to press out a damp, fleshy kiss. I felt slightly repelled. Wasn't I supposed to feel the opposite? Something was wrong with me. He's a man. I'm a woman. So aren't I supposed to feel something . . . something at least slightly passionate?

My hand yearned to vigorously scrub off his imprint, but instead I reached for the door handle. "Thanks for a lovely evening."

This time he came down on my lips with such force that I felt my own teeth cut against the inside flesh of my mouth. "I really have to be going along," I said, tasting blood, but experiencing concern that I was not feeling what Edna Louise and *Modern Romances* said I should be.

He didn't seem to hear. With all his strength, he was

busily pulling me toward him. I hated that and I hated his breathing which was becoming heavier and more insistent. With my free hand I pressed down on the handle and the door swung open. "Well, Marshall," I said, dragging myself out. "It sure has been a lovely evening."

· 7 ·

THE MORNING SMELLS from my Grandmother's Sunday
kitchen drifted into the guest bedroom carrying with them
a message of love and well-being. Impossible! Aromas, no
matter how devious, don't go wandering up a flight of stairs
and down a long hall to pass through the closed door of a
bedroom. And yet, there it was: beef fry frying (Edna
Louise once called it Jewish bacon), real honest perked
coffee, and the most glorious scent of them all, yeast. Yeast

raising bread or bialys or maybe even cheese and onion knishes. My favorite!

As I entered the kitchen, Grandpa looked up from his multisectioned *Commercial Appeal* which was spread out on the gray Formica-topped table in the breakfast nook. But it was Grandmother who spoke. "So tell us a little something about the rhapsodic dance. And about the *boychik*— uh . . . "

"Marshall Lubin."

"Yes, Marshall Lubin," agreed Grandma so rapidly and with such emphasis that it was as though she wanted credit for coming up with the right name. "So did he like you?"

Right off, I didn't exactly love her question. It smacked of: I'm selling something which Marshall may or may not decide to buy. "I didn't ask him, Grandmother, but I wish . . . I wish that you'd first please ask me if I liked him." At least, if he's going to show me up as a social klutz by not calling me again, then I'd like everybody to know that the chances are excellent that I'm not going to fall into an extended period of mourning. There'll be no sitting *shiva* for you, Mr. Lubin.

"So . . . well . . . " Grandma was smiling expectantly, as though I were about to confide something that she very much wanted to hear. "Did you like him?"

"Oh . . . he's okay, I guess," I said, noticing that my grandfather seemed every bit as interested as his wife. "But he doesn't possess even an echo of Sammy Fried's charm!"

Grandpa smiled as though fending off flattery while letting Grandma answer.

"For a husband there's still time," she said with such haste that I wondered if she didn't really mean that there was almost no time at all. I know she was only sixteen when she married, but that was a long time ago.

Anyway, I'm too sensitive. I know that. Not many other girls would be bothered by her question or think that they were being pushed into marriage. But I do believe that my own parents, for sure, would like to see me married as soon as possible. It's as though I'm some kind of disease which can only be cured by legally passing it on to somebody else.

Somehow, my father and maybe my mother too, got this notion that I'm oversexed and that any moment now I'm going to present them with a bastard grandchild. I feel so ashamed for being the kind of person that makes them believe that. Why me? Me, of all people! And yet I wouldn't even give them the satisfaction of telling them just how pure—speak about your Ivory soap—I am. Where, I'd really like to know, did my father get the idea that I was sexually voracious?

Because if anybody is always oogling up to the opposite sex, it's him. Not me!

Another thing that I don't begin to understand is why my mother continues to make routine (and altogether negative) evaluations regarding my attractiveness. Comments such as: "No wonder boys don't like you. You don't even bother to curl your hair." Or her other lament, "Why can't you put on a little charm for the boys?"

Well, my question is that since she's so damned aware of how unpopular I am, wouldn't you think she'd, at the very least, encourage my father to give me credit for purity? I mean being a sexual siren doesn't quite jibe with being socially backward. Neither in Jenkinsville nor in Memphis in this the year of our Lord 1950.

Now Edna Louise, whom my father has called "a perfect lady," may look like a cross between Snow White and Shirley Temple, but let me tell you she's not. No matter how much her parents and even mine may need to believe that. Why, the boys don't go around calling her "tasty tits" for nothing!

When I reached for my second cheese and onion knish, Grandma smiled as though I had bestowed upon her a great compliment. "They're terrific," I told her, just before biting into the most oniony part.

She filled my still half-filled cup with very hot coffee and asked, "You have something planned, something you want to do this afternoon?"

"There's a concert at the auditorium at two. Yehudi Menuhin."

Her senses seemed heightened. "Is the *boychik* taking you?"

Poor Grandmother is about to be disappointed. "Well, no . . ."

"Oh, somebody else maybe? Somebody you met last night at the club?"

"Nobody's taking me, Grandmother. I was planning to go alone."

I watched her try to hide her disappointment by smiling at me as though now that she thinks about it, going alone is the only really sensible thing to do.

After the concert I walked back down Main Street toward the Fortas Furniture Store where I had carefully maneuvered Grandma's Buick. I thought about the pleasure she gave me when she pressed her car keys into my palm. She had said simply, "Enjoy." The act itself seemed to represent those more important things that people never get around to saying—you're grown, you're trusted, you're loved.

I didn't mention it to her, but I did question the wisdom of letting an inexperienced driver behind the wheel of an unfamiliar car in a still unfamiliar city. Now, I don't want to pick on her or her judgment. Personally, I don't think there's anything wrong with letting me borrow her expensive car, but my father—boy, would he ever have a different idea!

For twenty minutes or so, I followed Jackson Avenue east until I came to the old stone gates with the bronze marker, Hein Park. I made a right turn onto Cypress Drive, driving down the narrow, winding roads heavy with summer foliage, past houses of history and elegance.

At the freshly white Victorian with the yellow-and-white striped window awnings, I executed a skillful turn into the blue asphalt driveway. A place like this had to do more than merely keep a person sheltered. 'Cause inside a home like this, you'd be more than warm and dry, you'd be protected from all manner of things.

Inside the garage, I cut the ignition and sat staring at the wall. I thought about Uncle Ben, Uncle Irv, and my mother, especially Mother. And I got to wondering what was it really like for them growing up in this house. What bothers me is the thought that if my mother had gotten something from this house, from her parents, wouldn't she be able—wouldn't she just insist upon giving something back to me?

This was, after all, the place where my mother learned that her spectacular looks were worthy of the world's homage. And maybe that's when and why my grandparents became confused and eventually couldn't tell the difference between Pearl's wants and Pearl's needs. Is that why my mother knows so much more about taking than giving?

Just the same my grandparents didn't mean harm. I know that! Maybe it was only that they tried too hard to protect their sons and daughter from those across-the-Atlantic Polish soldiers and all other evils either known or imagined by man.

And it's these thoughts that keep burning at me, interfering at times with my feeling for my grandparents. Like last Friday—Thursday, it must have been. I was trying to figure out why their own children didn't turn out all that well and while I was thinking, Grandmother said something to me and I answered her so sharply that right before my eyes, I saw my own grandmother shrink into an aged child.

I chased away some black sheep thoughts, but they kept edging back. I don't care what the black sheep says—my grandparents are good people! And they were the best parents that they knew how to be.

And there's something else you sheep must remember: With people, it's not just what is given that counts. It's also how what is given is received.

· 8 ·

ON TUESDAY, the last morning of my Memphis visit, I
walked into the kitchen before eight. Grandmother waved
in my direction, but continued to speak directly into the
phone. "Wait a minute. Patty just came downstairs. I'll ask
her."

She held the receiver between her breasts. "Patty, it's your
Aunt Dorothy. Her best friend, Lois Glazer, has a daughter
your age who's having an open house tonight."

She then directed her comments into the phone. "What's the daughter's name? . . . Yes, Iris . . . Iris Glazer . . . I'm sure Patty would love to go. . . . Such a nice place to make friends."

Of all life's possibilities one of the most unappealing, ranking only a hairline notch above being left to drown in a vat of pure castor oil, would be going alone to a stranger's party. "Let me speak to her, please," I said, taking the receiver. "Listen, Aunt Dorothy, I really appreciate your thinking about me and I'd really love to go, but I simply must get back to Jenkinsville tonight. But thanks an awful lot anyway."

Before the receiver reached its cradle, Grandmother intercepted, wearing a look of intense disappointment. "I don't know why you have to rush back there. Haven't you had a good time with us? We tried to give you a good time."

"I had a wonderful time, Grandmother. Honest!"

"So why the rush? What kind of business, *Gottenyu,* do you have there? Among the *goyim*?"

I tried to think of something to tell her, something that made sense. "Well," I said, falling back on the truth, "I do work in the store, you know. Keeps my parents from having to hire extra help."

Grandma bit her lower lip as though it were a pocket that suddenly needed buttoning. "Let your daddy and mother earn the living." Then she nodded her head as though to convince herself that she was only doing right. "Let them at least do that for you."

I knew that she'd paid some sort of price, made some sort of sacrifice for those words and I wanted to reward them. "Okay, Grandmother, if you think I should."

And from that it apparently seemed clear to her that I was not only going to leave the burden of making a living to my parents, but that I had also contracted to go to the open house tonight. Exactly when and where did I say that?

Grandma was dialing the long-distance operator. "Would you please be so kindly as to put this call through to number seventy-eight in Jenkinsville, Arkansas? . . . Harry? . . . Hello there, Harry. Is that you, Harry? Good . . . Everything good? . . . *Gott'danken* . . . You got your health you got everything. . . . Is Pearl there? Oh, she's got a customer. . . . So okay, I'll tell you, Harry. There's a party here that Patty's dying to go to, wants to stay over an extra day."

Moments later, she pressed the phone against herself and gave me an affirmative nod. "Your daddy says he doesn't care how long you stay."

We left the house before eleven to do, on this last full day of my visit, all the things we hadn't as yet done: We saw the shopping center under construction out on Poplar Avenue and Grandma drove over every inch of Memphis State College.

At two o'clock we ate a real pit barbecue sandwich at Leonard's. People who ought to know say that nowhere else in this country can you get a barbecue like a Leonard's Pit barbecue. The meat itself is so smokily spiced that it's practically guaranteed to clear out your nasal passages for life. And if you're willing to pay the price to be a hero in your own time, then sprinkle the meat liberally with pepper sauce. Volcanic!

About eight thirty in the evening, Grandma brought the car to a stop in front of a long, fieldstone house where (damn the kilowatts and full power ahead) every conceivable light (both inside and outside) burned. There was no stinting with the music either. Everybody all up and down Cypress Drive could hear every note, every word.

> *Arrivederci Roma* . . .
> *Goodbye* . . . *Goodbye to Rome* . . .

For some moments, Grandma listened with me before leaning over to kiss me goodnight and goodbye. "I know you'll have a wonderful time at . . . "

"Iris Glazer's," I supplied.

"Iris Glazer's," Grandmother repeated. "Her mother is a close friend of your Aunt Dorothy's."

"I know," I said, wondering how far that could take me, while Grandmother smiled as though already anticipating my "wonderful time." For wanting that for me, I think I loved her; for pushing me here tonight, I think I hated her.

I dashed up the Glazers' front walk as though I couldn't wait to arrive, until I heard the Buick drive off. Then I came to an abrupt stop. Bringing as much Cypress Drive air into my lungs as possible, I adjusted my peasant blouse and my full ballerina skirt before slowly climbing up the three or four terrazzo steps to press a tremorous index finger against the button.

The door was opened by a slim girl with cheekbones like an Apache. She gave me a sort of who-the-hell-are-you look. "Hi, I'm Patty Bergen," I said, and when her quizzical stare showed no sign of fading, I continued, "My aunt, Dorothy Fried, is a friend of your mother's."

79

"Oh," she said, opening the door barely wide enough for me to enter the overly air-conditioned house. "I'm Iris," said Iris Glazer, already moving away to re-enter her tight circle of friends.

Gliding across the highly polished floor of the living room, bobby-soxed girls pressed against brightly shirted boys.

> *Save your loving arms for my returning . . .*
> *Keep the flame of love still burning . . .*
> *Within my heart . . . Oh, arrivederci Roma . . .*

As I looked around the room for another single of either sex to join, I felt about as graceful as Bull Durham among the swans. There was something about being a stranger—and maybe even something more about being a single among plurals. I wondered if even old Noah would have known what to do with me. Would he have been able to find somebody to walk with me up that gangplank?

On the buffet table, red candles dripped intricate trails down straw-wrapped Chianti bottles, while a red-and-white-checkered tablecloth played background to some great-looking food. There were cold cuts of all kinds, a chafing dish filled with spaghetti and meat balls, and a Jell-O mold so spectacular that it came in three colors and combined more varieties of fruit than I was able to identify.

As I helped myself to a good-sized helping of it and the spaghetti, I told myself that if I had more pride, I would refuse (absolutely!) to eat where I wasn't welcome. Umm . . . this is spaghetti! But Iris didn't exactly not welcome me. And there's nothing wrong with this Jell-O either.

Maybe it was she who was offended when I didn't follow

80

her over to her encampment. Well, if she had wanted me, wouldn't she have said, "Come on over and meet my friends?" Or "I'd like to introduce you to . . . " You know, Patty Bergen, you amaze me, you really do. You who are always wanting people to be nice to you! Well, why don't you sometimes try being nice to others? Give to them. Extend yourself. Bread upon the waters and all that.

With my back propped against the wall, I ate slowly while making plans to assault Iris Glazer's citadel. But how? With some startling piece of information. Such as? Oh, such as: Memphis should have had more people attending Yehudi Menuhin's concert. In a city of three hundred and fifty thousand, barely two hundred roused themselves to go listen to a world-famous violinist!

Classify that under important, but not generally conceived of as important. Startling! I need something startling. Well, I could comment on the random mix of architecture at Memphis State College and how it gives the place an unplanned, almost haphazard look. I sighed. Use same classification as previously indicated.

At the opposite corner of the room, five people had turned expectant faces toward Iris. "Well, after I refused Melvin a date," she told them, "for three straight Saturday nights do you know what that jerk did? He sent me one of those mushy greeting cards that said thinking of you. M. That's how he signed it. Just M."

At last poor Melvin scores. He makes everybody laugh. Not so much laugh as snicker. Some citadel! This is what I'm so anxious to enter? Damn right! It sure beats standing here all alone. Okay, okay. But where's all the startling stuff that's going to pay the entrance fee?

Don't go thinking I don't have something that would make Iris Glazer's Melvin story sound like a retelling of Goldilocks. And what big teeth you have, Grandma! Why, I could tell them about myself. Hear ye . . . hear ye! I, a guest of this beautiful house, am about to make a confession of startling consequence, but first lock up your valuables and hide your weapons. Because, ladies and gentlemen, you now see before you—tah-dah!—a genuine, appearing in person . . . ex-con!

Suddenly I'd be the hub of Iris's cluster and soon neighboring clusters would swell the original one until everybody here belonged to a single cluster: mine. Each and every single one of them would be burning to know about me. "What's your favorite weapon? Have you ever robbed a bank? Killed anyone recently?"

I placed my now empty plate on the edge of the buffet table knowing that I would never willingly swap my permanent isolation for instant notoriety. It's not that I'm convinced that isolation is somehow better or less painful. It's only that I guess it's . . . more familiar.

As though it were a very natural thing to do, I headed toward the circle that belonged to Iris. Between two guys there was room for maybe half a body, so using my shoulder as a wedge, part of me became very definitely part of the Iris group while more than half of me definitely wasn't.

When our hostess saw me (and she did see me), I hoped that she'd say something welcoming. Maybe introduce me to her friends, but first we had to wait until the fellow wearing white bucks finished telling his joke about the sailor and the movie star who are stranded alone on this desert island. When that joke finally ended, I laughed with the others. Make believe you're having a wonderful time. WHEEEeee . . . ! ! !

Then Iris (and I don't understand how this linked in with the previous conversation) said, "Everybody says that the University of Texas sorority girls are the most beautiful in the world."

Was opportunity finally knocking for me? "I'm seriously considering," I told her, "going to the University of Texas. Do you think it's a good school?"

Her eyes checked me over as though I were a raw recruit standing inspection. "That depends," she answered, while her elbow poked into the ribs of the girl next to her. And the girl, as if on cue, fell into syncopated laughter with Iris. I waited for them to explain further. I waited . . . wanting so much to join Iris and her pal inside the laughter.

But instead I watched the two girls as they began supporting each other from the pure debilitating effects. What were they doing? Ridiculing me? People who live in fine houses don't ridicule their guests, do they? Maybe I accidentally said something funny. Maybe in just another moment, they'll apologize for excluding me and then explain with real patience and kindness exactly what it is that's so hysterically funny.

I asked, "What's so funny?"

"Nothing you'd be interested in," said Iris while falling into a still more acute attack of snickered laughter. "Nothing at all."

Face the truth. I am not wanted. That much is clear. I looked directly at her and spoke in deliberate tones. "Thank you for inviting me to your party, Iris."

Before I turned away, I saw that my hostess had lost every last ounce of her laughter. As I walked through the front door, there were two things I carried with me that kept my humiliation from being complete.

Somewhere above Iris's haughty cheekbones, I had caught something surprised, almost frightened, by my response. And then there was that other thing: Beneath her pale silk blouse her breasts were flat as matzohs.

When I left the air-conditioned house, the night struck me with its heavy warmth. I walked the narrow parklike turns of Cypress Drive knowing only that I had to be somewhere else. Someplace where nobody could see me . . . or call my name.

All I know is that growing up hurts too much. Growing down is what I'd really like to do. Be little enough again so that it would be perfectly natural to be protected from the wind and the rain—and the world.

By the time I crossed North Parkway to enter a restaurant called The Cotton Boll, the soles of my feet were burning because it was well past midnight and I had already walked too long. I bought a pack of filter-tip cigarettes from the cashier and gave the waitress my order for a barbecue (dark meat only) and a cup of coffee.

The coffee comforted me somewhat while the sandwich encouraged me to believe that my ability to enjoy hadn't been permanently destroyed, but only temporarily impaired. And I think I'm almost steady enough now to lay it all out. Look at what happened tonight and why.

First, I didn't do anything wrong. Nothing that I'm ashamed of. I wondered if Iris Glazer could make that same statement. Remembering that none of the guys and only that one girl who was trying hard to be Iris's mirror-image joined in the attack, I wondered how she could justify it to the rest of them. More important, how can she justify it to herself? 'Cause isn't it desirable, even for girls with impervious cheekbones, to like themselves?

Suddenly I caught a glimpse at what might have been a truth and I wanted to share my findings with Melvin. The Melvin of mushy-greeting-card fame. "Oh, Melvin," I'd tell him. "You don't have a thing in this world to be ashamed of."

With love you reached out for somebody else. Sure, she laughed, but maybe that was only because she understood one thing you didn't: That within Iris Glazer, there is precious little worth loving.

THE NEXT MORNING, Grandma asked the predictable question. "I heard you come in after one o'clock. You had a good time?"

"Oh, very nice, thank you."

"See," she said, smiling as though being right had left a delicious taste in her mouth. "Now, aren't you glad you listened to your grandmother? Stayed over an extra day to go to the party? How did you get home?"

" . . . Well, Roderick took me."

Her face looked uncertain. "Roderick? What kind of a name is that? Not a Yiddisher?"

"Why, Grandmother," I said, acting as though my integrity was being questioned. "Sure, he is. Why, he's practically a dentist!"

"That's nice. They're almost as good as real doctors."

I wanted to retreat from my lie. "Well, he's not sure, though. He still may decide to become something else."

She showed surprise. It was as though the very next best thing to clipping brain tumors was pulling molars and if Roderick didn't understand that, there was something a little shaky about his sanity.

Suddenly I wanted to defend him from her unfair and unfounded suspicions. "It's not as simple a decision as you may think. You see, Roderick's got this phobia about people's mouths. He admitted to me (and only to me) that he's deathly afraid that one of his patients might . . . bite him!"

But when I saw Grandma gently shaking her head, I knew that I had only worsened it. "That's nonsense," she said. "A real *mishegoss*."

"You know," I told her, "that's exactly what I told him."

At one o'clock in the afternoon, after much insisting from me: "I will feel absolutely terrible if you miss your Mah-Jongg game on account of me." And her counter-arguments: "After twenty-five years of Mah-Jongg, is it such a terrible crime to spend the last day of my granddaughter's visit with her?"

Finally she wearied of arguing and so trailing a scent of Chanel No. 5, she left for Ida Baum's. And, for the first time ever, I had complete freedom of the house. But I didn't feel free. Not a bit! Who could while being padlocked deep within the intrusive and compulsive confines of an obsession?

Just off the lobby of the Peabody Hotel was the American International Travel Agency. While still on the lobby side of the plate glass, I studied the dramatic interior with its electric blue rug woven with the A.I.T.A. logo over a fast-whirling globe.

The personnel consisted of two men and a woman each sitting at a walnut desk shaped like the top of an aircraft carrier and topped by two telephones. The longer I looked, the more I was certain that they shared something besides identical office equipment, for they each emanated a sort of "take-charge" quality.

"No, madam, we do not recommend Casablanca in March. The high winds from nearby dunes make it impossible to enjoy a cup of tea with anything that approaches sandless serenity."

Abruptly I closed my eyes against all distractions. Pursue the obsession, I commanded myself, or ditch it. Ditch it now. You can't have it both ways, nobody can. And here only an arm's reach from the American International Travel Agency is the perfect spot to jettison forever this embarrassing and impractical dream. For me to chase a ridiculous compulsion across an alien continent would be too upsetting for both my parents and my grandparents. Isn't it possible—can't I, at least, try to become the kind of daughter and grand-daughter that they would like?

Somebody has got to get it through my head that Hans

Christian Andersen and a few others may have written fairy tales, but almost nobody has ever lived one. Please . . . please . . . before it's too late, give it up. For everybody's sake, please give it up now! Because the truth is, it doesn't make any sense—not even to me!

I don't know if I can give up what I need so much. Anyway, I don't know how to become the perfect daughter and granddaughter. Wouldn't even begin to know how to conform to some idealized specifications that are locked deep within the hearts and minds of others. Even Grandmother's pattern which was carefully prepared for me with a large quantity of love doesn't come anywhere close to fitting me. She, for example, certainly didn't figure on my social ineptitude or Iris Glazer's arrogant inhospitality. Maybe we all have to learn custom tailoring for ourselves.

I opened my eyes to look again at the round polished brass of the doorknob, but what I saw was my own hand reaching out, reaching out for it. Okay, okay! So go. But don't you dare come crying back to me when things go exploding in your face. Don't you dare come crying back to me. Do you hear?

I turned; it clicked. It made a decisive sound.

· 10 ·

ORDINARILY, I would have suggested house shoes after Mrs. Hester Rhodes bought the pink-and-white seersucker robe, but it was getting close to two o'clock and my father is just unpredictable enough suddenly to take it upon himself to go striding in his fastest firehouse gait down to the post office for the afternoon mail. God forbid!

Of course, sooner or later he's got to know. Sooner or later, I'll have to break it to them. But in the meantime, I don't want him to present me with a letter from either the passport office or the travel agency. If that happened, I'd be too rattled from fright even to try to explain why I'm going to Europe. What could I possibly tell him that would help him understand?

Try telling him that Paris may be the greatest cultural capital of all time. Known throughout the world for its architecture, museums, theaters. If my sense of humor weren't consumed by raw fear, I would have laughed. Imagine telling that to my father!

Without bothering to ask the widow Rhodes if there would be anything else, I counted back change from a five-dollar bill and while almost running toward the front door called out, "Come again."

The double box numbered 1010 was stuffed. I twirled the dial clockwise, counterclockwise, and finally clockwise until the catch released. The magazine *Modern Retailer* was wrapped around a batch of business letters, and the second one was addressed to me. And there it was: the A.I.T.A. letters emblazoned across a whirling globe. With trembling hands and an overexcited heart, I tore into the envelope and allowed myself a close-to-the-body peek. A typed ticket read: S.S. *Ryndam* (Holland-America) lv N.Y. Sept 15, 1950 arrv LeHavre, France Sept 22, 1950.

As soon as I re-entered the store, I could see that the Saturday rush was on. All it takes is a truckload or two of Mexicans. Our local farmers have been having to import more and more of them for seasonal work ever since World War II when the Negroes began moving to places like Detroit and Chicago. They're getting jobs in manufacturing plants for as much as forty dollars a week which doesn't take into account the overtime.

Funny thing is I can't remember hearing anybody from around here ever saying a decent word about Negroes until they started moving away. Use to always call them lazy, no-good, and shiftless. Now the white farmers are constantly saying things like, "I have to hire me seventy-five wetbacks to do the work of fifty niggers." And there's that other widely spoken compliment: "At least when the niggers talked you could understand them."

According to my father, though, the biggest problem with the Mexicans is that practically none of their earned money ever sees the light of morn until it crosses the Mexican border. "A Mex just won't spend a nickel in this country that he doesn't have to," said my father to Mr. Bert Oliver who owns the Sav-mor Market, "while the Negro, on the other hand, worked from sunup to sundown to earn a dollar, and an hour after the sun went down he was already ten cents in debt."

But I guess if you're honest then you can find something about everybody that's worth bragging about. I could even brag about my father, if I wanted to. He's a really sharp dresser and he's more democratic than the other merchants, who seem to operate on the principle that the richer you are, the better discount you deserve.

Once, for example, I was with Edna Louise when she stopped by the Sav-mor for a package of Hydrox cookies, and since she didn't have her purse, I offered to lend her the money till she got home. She laughed an all-knowing laugh. "Don't be silly. We get the same discount whether we pay cash or charge."

Well, I'm proud to say that my father has the same ticket-marked price for everybody, and it's not all that easy either 'cause even if this is Bergen's Department Store's twentieth-anniversary year, I still hear the more well-to-do customers asking my father to "knock a little off, Harry."

He's a regular incorruptible though, 'cause he's always giving them the same response. "I wouldn't knock anything off, not even if you were my mother-in-law. And specially not if you were my mother-in-law!"

What I like best about him is that sometimes I'll overhear him tell a story which reminds me that, at least for others, he can exhibit a real sense of humor. I guess that's also what I dislike about him. I mean why is it that he can show good things to others—fairness and a democratic spirit to his customers, a sense of humor to the proprietor of the Sav-mor, and compliments to the most overcomplimented girl in Jenkinsville—but can give nothing to me? Nothing good to me!

As soon as my father saw me, he yelled across the breadth of the store, "Patricia!" I thought he wanted to know about the mail, so I called back, "I left it in the usual place. On the side of the register."

But he only yelled again, "Come here."

"Yes, sir." I walked as quickly as I could without actually breaking into a run. I wouldn't want him to ever suspect that he scares me. The problem is that I don't know when he's going to be set off. Sometimes he explodes over almost nothing. Something that nobody could have ever predicted.

Like a week ago Sunday when my mother tried to force me to wear that blouse that Uncle Irv and Aunt Dorothy gave me for Chanukah. It was my least favorite color, orchid; my least favorite fabric, rayon; and my least favorite style, tiny cone-shape buttons marching in single-filed monotony up to the very top of its lacy peter-pan collar.

And since nobody could ever accuse my father of trying to please either his wife or his in-laws, I was shocked when he came butting into the argument. "If you don't put that blouse on," he shouted, "I'm going to beat the living hell out of you."

When I went into my room to put on the blouse, he stood just outside my closed door yelling about how I get so much I don't appreciate a thing. "Not a goddamn thing! 'Cause you've been spoiled rotten since the day you were born. I work my head off to give you things that my daddy could never afford to give *me*!"

I mentally catalogued my extravagances: some lovely new clothes that Grandma bought me, a twenty-five-dollar dictionary (also from Grandmother), an eight-year-old bike, membership in both the Book-of-the-Month Club and the Literary Guild, and a Parker pen and pencil set. Are those the things that my father wants and resents my having? Dummy, he could afford to buy any and all of those things . . . but still he does resent something. Only if it's nothing more than my having a father who could give me things that his could never afford.

I sat on my bed looking at the hateful blouse and remembered what it was that Uncle Irv once said about his wife: "Dorothy would buy a truckload of manure if she got the notion that it was a bargain." Well, thanks a bunch, Aunt Dorothy.

At eighteen, I may be legally an adult, but now that his will and pride were involved, there was no way, absolutely no way, that I could get away without wearing that thing.

. . . Unless of course, the blouse was in some way . . . indecent. This blouse indecent? Why, my God, that collar would hug my throat the way a reformed sinner would hug his Bible. But if I could make this indecent, then it would become a battle between his need for absolute obedience—Heil Hitler—and his need to keep me in perfect purity—Hail Mary!

With a razor blade, I ever so imperceptibly lengthened the buttonholes until now with only the slightest of pressure, the conical-shaped button jumped through the opening.

I went into the living room where they were both engrossed in the thick Sunday *Commercial Appeal*. They looked up: My mother was actually wearing a pleasant expression. "Now, aren't you ashamed of all the fuss you've made? I don't believe I've ever seen you looking so nice. And you know, your Uncle Irv and Aunt Dorothy are going to be as pleased as punch."

"Yes, but I'm not pleased, Mother. Actually, I'm very upset that you would sacrifice my pleasure for theirs," I said, filling my lungs and watching the "trained" buttons obediently pop through their holes.

Above unfathomable depths of contempt, my mother wore a rice-paper-thin covering of pretended civility. "It won't hurt you to make a sacrifice once in a while for your uncle and aunt. Your blouse came unbuttoned."

"Oh, you know how cheaply these blouses are made," I said with just about the right amount of surprised innocence, while watching my father cringing beneath the mid-South news pages. See no evil.

What, I wondered, are you really seeing? All those girls

95

that you've taken advantage of? Once, I remember, your brother Max was saying that no man understood women, and then he had a second thought. Gave you some gentle jabs to the ribs to say, "Well, maybe a few alley cats like you, Harry!"

Minutes later when we were ready to leave for Memphis, my father told me to check that the back door was securely locked.

I filled every available lung space with air as I nonchalantly pulled back my elbows. "Want me to latch the screen door, too?"

His eyes caught themselves on the fleshy part of my breast that spilled over my bra. "Er—yes! Lock that, too."

"Yes, sir," I answered, heading toward the kitchen door.

"And if you can't keep that blouse buttoned," he called out, "then put something else on, understand?"

"Yes, sir," I answered, careful to hide my pleasure. "I understand." But I don't understand why you get so upset about things like that, not really. Unless, it's that you're so afraid that some boy is going to do to me what you've already done to so many girls.

But that was then and what I'm worried about now is what he could possibly want, standing in the middle of the store, yelling my name. It couldn't have anything to do with my boat ticket to Europe because there was absolutely, positively nobody in that post office and even if there was, I only allowed myself a few quick peeks within the envelope before hiding it deep inside my skirt pocket.

He was impatiently watching a particularly short Mexican who pointed toward the toes of his dusty huaraches saying, "Parche . . . parche, para callo."

My father responded by pointing to his highly polished black brogues saying, "Zapato . . . zapato?"

At which point the migrant worker waved his finger in brisk windshield-wiper fashion to repeat, "No, señor, no zapato. Gracias. Parche! Parche! Parche para callo."

Bending over slightly to lift the leg of his trouser, my father pinched the top of his black socks and almost pleadingly asked, "Socks? Men's socks?"

Again the windshield wiper which monitored his head movements was set into motion. "No, no, señor. Gracias."

My father shot me a desperate look which meant that I was to take over now which was all right with me since I had an idea. I asked, "Tiene malos los pies?"

Suddenly he lit up as though he had just received a package from home. "Sí, señorita. Sí!"

After I had sold him a package of Dr. Scholl's small corn pads, I found my father. "You know, I've been thinking. It wouldn't be a bad idea if you'd let Miss Cox at the high school give all us clerks a simple Spanish course. She's probably the best teacher I've ever had."

He waved me away. "Don't let these Españols kid you. If they want to, they can speak our language better'n we can."

"I don't understand why everybody in this town insists on saying that! Have you ever tried learning somebody else's language?"

He bellowed out cigarette smoke along with his answer. "When I say something, I don't want it contradicted. Understand?"

"But I wasn't! I was just giving you my opinion . . . from experience. Why does my opinion always bother you?"

The pupils of his eyes looked as though they were made

97

out of a guaranteed unbreakable substance. "Don't you ever make the mistake of thinking you're too big for me to knock the living hell out of."

I stood there facing him with unusually impeccable posture, resisting the terrible temptation to step back, lower my head, cast my eyes downward or in any one of a dozen ways transmit a signal of surrender.

I was standing there, not completely certain that I was going to escape injury, when it came to me that maybe my father had inadvertently given me the reason why I hadn't had "the living hell" beaten out of me for going on five years. Now that I think of it, I doubt that he's touched me for any reason in all that time. What were his secret fears?

"You answer me!"

That was always necessary for my father—insisting that I verbalize my defeat while proclaiming his victory. Wouldn't you think he'd know he had won without having to be told.

I offered him an expressionless face. "I don't know what it is you want me to say."

"Say, yes, sir. It won't happen again."

"Yes, sir. It won't happen again."

"And say you're sorry."

"And I'm sorry," I repeated, hoping he could catch just that quality in my voice which made it sound as though my words had been processed through some very large and impersonal machine.

• 11 •

AUGUST THE FIFTEENTH was the last, final, absolute deadline that I gave myself. By August 15, I had to break it to them that I was going to Europe. Today, August 15, 1950, I woke with a heavy head and a deep sense of impending disaster.

Although for a month now I had been practicing telling them, practicing a dozen different approaches, there wasn't one of them that I thought they'd even remotely understand, much less approve of. I told myself that it wasn't going to be pleasant, but I was strong. I could live through unpleasantness if only I could remember two things: Sticks and stones still don't break bones, and there is nothing in this world that they can do to stop me.

At precisely six o'clock, Sarita called out, "SUP-per!" and my father, mother, Sharon, and I sat down at the flowered-cloth covered table to pot roast, collards, crowder peas, cornbread, and iced tea in tall festive glasses.

As my father sliced himself a perfectly enormous cut of the pot roast, my mother spoke about how we just have to do something. "I'd run a good-sized ad in the *Rice County Gazette*."

"Years ago," said my father, "I told Quent when he came around looking to sell ads that I'd rather use my money for toilet paper. Least thataways, it wouldn't be a total loss."

Sharon laughed at what must be his all-time favorite joke while my mother went on talking. "Tell jokes if you want to, Harry, but remember half of August is already gone and we're way over-inventoried on summer shoes."

Sharon bent toward me, whispering about what happened to Arlene Rosen at the recent BBG conclave in Nashville. "Her period came two days early and she didn't have anything but an old gym sock to use."

She laughed a mischievous laugh and I joined in, but not because I found it funny, which I didn't. If anything, I found both Sharon's and my father's suppertime talk slightly offensive, but you can't go by me, 'cause I'm kinda prudish. Or at least Edna Louise thinks so.

But offensive stories or not, I generally like having Sharon around. For one thing, she's both very pretty and very sweet which makes me think that I'm mistaken about my parents. Maybe I'm too harsh on them and they're really not all that bad. Else how could they have had her?

"I brought you some fingernail polish from the store," she said, whipping it from the back pocket of her plaid shorts. "It's a new shade. Like you like. See, not too bright."

"Why do you always want to polish my nails, Sharon? I wouldn't want to polish yours."

"Don't you know," she giggled, "it's fun to make things pretty. Will you let me?"

"No, last time you did my nails, you didn't have any remover to clean up the mistakes."

With dazzling orange-tipped fingers, Sharon reached back into her hip pocket and brought forth a full bottle of yellow nail-polish remover.

I looked again at the bottle of Rose Dust polish and was about to give Sharon my half-hearted permission, when I heard my mother use my name.

"What are you saying about me?"

"Nothing. It was nothing."

"What do you mean nothing? I heard you use my name."

My mother sighed as though I were inexcusably slowing her down. "I was telling your daddy that we oughta write the William R. Moore Company, the Memphis Wholesale Mart, and Cantor & Sons to establish a credit rating for you."

It sounded decidedly important and flattering too. But why would I need a credit rating? Right off, I thought of one possibility that made sense. If my parents were suddenly killed in, say, an automobile accident, then who else but I would take care of Sharon? Run the store? I felt saddened as though their deaths were imminent and yet I also felt enormously pleased. Never would I have guessed that they'd have that kind of confidence in me. And I'm not going to let them down either. They can depend on that!

My father was pointing an index finger at me as though directing his words to their destination in the centermost core of my brain. "If I call you up and tell you to go down to a certain jobber for a gross of men's work socks, then I don't want you to take it upon yourself to buy another thing. Understand?"

"Yes, sir," I answered, not really understanding at all. "Do you maybe sometimes want me to go into Memphis for you? Do a little buying for the store?"

"No, not till you're there."

"Sir?"

"Not now," he said. "Not until you're already there in the dormitory at Teacher's Normal."

My mother interjected. "They don't call it 'Teacher's Normal' anymore, Harry. They haven't for years. It's Memphis State College now."

"Wait a minute," I said. "Wait a minute!" I felt the familiar onrush of rage for having my life controls snatched from me. "What are you all thinking? That I'm going there? To Memphis State College?"

My father blinked and I knew that inadvertently he had given it all away. The controls of my life were back in my hands where they belonged. "Isn't that where you want to go?" he asked. "It's cheap and it's near home."

"Oh, no, sir," I answered. "That's not at all where I want to go."

"Well, where do you want to go?"

Without hesitation, I said the word. Heard myself say the word, "Europe," and I was so busy congratulating myself on my freshly found courage that I wasn't, wasn't at this moment, frightened.

"What!" shouted my father, and unless I'm mistaken my mother shouted it, too.

"Well," I said, knowing that after these next sentences left my mouth, "normal" would be a long time coming. "After much thought, I've decided to spend my own money—the thousand dollars that Grandmother and Grandfather gave me—going on a little tour of Europe. When I come back, you won't have to worry. I'll work part time and go to college part time. I won't be a burden! I'll pay my own way. I promise!"

"Who ever heard of such a thing!" screamed my mother. "Who goes there? Nobody. Only soldiers to fight! Where does she get those ideas? She doesn't get them from me. So where?"

My father turned his attention and his comments toward her. "Calm down, Pearl! Now calm yourself down! What Patricia says she's going to do and what she actually does is a horse of a different color. She's going to Europe like I'm going to fly a kite."

"I am going," I said flatly, and I caught something out of the corner of my eye. Sharon was sending me the message: DANGER, with only a quick shake of her head and a pained look on her face.

I gave my sister barely a nod, but I knew that she had read in it my own message of thanks for her reminder to proceed with extreme caution. "The whole thing is," I spoke directly to my parents, but I wondered if Sharon caught the new tone of conciliation in my voice, "that for an awful long time I've wanted to travel . . . see foreign places.

"Remember those movies, *Three Coins in the Fountain* and that other one—uh . . . *The Last Time I Saw Paris*? Know how many times I saw those films?" I could tell that this was no time to ask them to count movie stubs. "Well, I saw them each four times because I just love foreign scenery and now I want to see it for real! Can you understand that?"

My father jumped to his feet. On his face raged a fury so insane that I questioned his ability to control it, even with my grown-woman status. I sucked in every bit of air my lungs could accommodate and it wasn't until I saw my breasts swell that I understood why.

It must have worked, too, because while his rage was ongoing—"Well, unlike you and your kind, I love this country! I'd kill for this country!"—his potential for violence against me seemed to have subsided. "This is the greatest, most wonderful country on God's green earth and if you had"—he snapped his fingers as though snapping away dirt—"a single ounce of patriotism, then this family wouldn't have been ruined by your treason!"

So he's still with that, is he? Still with Anton. Well, let them be. What do I care? Sticks and stones. I'm not upset. It's practically exactly what I expected. Sticks and stones . . . sticks and— I pressed an index finger against the point of burning, of icy burning just beneath my ribs. My head, my stomach began to revolve. Spinning faster and faster without benefit of a single control.

I got to my feet, slapping my hand across my mouth. To the bathroom. Fast! The room revolved then darkened without blackening. Never, not in my whole life, have I ever fainted. Wouldn't faint now.

As I threw open the bathroom door and positioned my head directly above the bowl, I heard my mother call my name. "Patricia, don't you dare puke on that floor!"

· 12 ·

FOR A WHOLE month now, and for the second time in my life, I've become Jenkinsville's number one topic of conversation. Edna Louise Jackson was one of the first people to ask me about it. "You really and truly intend to go to Paris, France?"

"Yes."

"Well, what in the world for?"

"It's hard to explain. I've always wanted to travel, you know, see things I've never—"

"My daddy told me that he heard that your daddy wrote you right out of his will."

"Really?" I lied. "I hadn't heard that." At least not since the previous night. But it isn't the threat of being disinherited that's so hard to bear, although someday if I'm poor and can't find work, it will be. The really hard thing is what he said to me on Wednesday after driving back in from Memphis.

"Patricia," he had said in a voice so calm that it was downright scary. "You oughta know that the real reason I went into Memphis today wasn't to buy goods for the store."

"Yes, sir," I answered, waiting for the inevitable verbal ax to come bisecting my brain.

"My main reason for going to Memphis was to have a talk, and I mean to tell you, I had a long talk with Rabbi Goodstein."

Rabbi Goodstein? The Rabbi Goodstein of weddings, High Holy Days, *beriths,* and Bar Mitzvahs? I searched for the connection. "Sir?"

"Disinheritance," said my father, speaking with inordinate slowness, "is too goddamn good for you. After what you've put this family through. The public disgrace with that Nazi and now . . . now this! This sneaking off to Europe."

"Sneaking is when you don't tell. I told. Please just remember that I told!"

My pleading voice, though, must have alerted my mother because she came into the room spewing large quantities of her own special brand of verbal kerosene. "Only reason girls from around here run off is when they have to get rid

107

of an illegitimate baby. Is *that* why you're going? You can tell the truth!"

"PEARL!" My father screamed and I could see that he had to restrain himself just to keep from killing her. "You GET the hell on out of here!"

My mother looked shocked that he was now turning his rage against her.

Doesn't she know better than that? Why, he can never even hear the mention of the word sex in front of me. Sometimes I think it's because he wants to keep me from something he knows I'll hate—or will love so much that I'll be in danger of becoming an alley cat too. But I don't want to think about that anymore.

After chasing Mother away, he came back with his sharply honed ax. "If you go off to Paris, I'm going to do exactly what I told Rabbi Goodstein I was going to do. For me, you will be dead, and for the dead I sit *shiva*. You leave, and I swear to God I'll recite the prayers of the dead over you."

"I also heard"—here Edna Louise allowed herself a little Jacksonian pause—"that your poor mother cries herself to sleep every night."

Now that was a bold-faced lie! My mother has never been known to keep her head aloft much beyond ten o'clock. "I hadn't heard that one either," I answered, grateful for at least the fact that not one of her questions connected up to Anton. "Well, what else have you heard?" I asked, thinking that France was, after all, a pretty good diversionary tactic.

"Oh . . . nothing much . . . only . . . "

"Only what?" Was the connection now going to be made?

"Only about those Frenchmen."

"What about them?"

Edna Louise narrowed the sidewalk space between us. "Well, I heard that they engage in unnatural sex."

My mind was filled with all kinds of questions because probably the closest that I've ever come to even natural sex was in the movies. It happened just during that period when Clark Gable kissed Loretta Young so hard out there on the balcony of her New York penthouse that the scene had nowhere to go decently, so in the name of decency it just fuzzed out.

Now, trying to find out the answer to the question that was agitating my brain would mean that I'd have to inform the world (via Edna Louise) just how ignorant I was about sex. Still I knew myself well enough to know that, caught between the fires of this agitating kind of curiosity and a somewhat less than devastating embarrassment, I'd probably opt to quench the curiosity. And so I did, but in a way that was hopefully calculated to convey the impression that I knew practically everything there is to know about the subject, but perhaps, I could accommodate just a bare molecule more.

And so while trying to conjure up the professorial image of Walter Pidgeon, I asked, "What specifically do you mean by unnatural sex?"

For one who had gained a reputation for having succulent nipples, Edna Louise began to look surprisingly uncomfortable. Finally her gaze seemed to re-focus as she said, "About the same thing, I reckon, that other people mean when they say"—her head moved toward my ear—"unnatural sex."

As I tried to figure out how in this world I am ever going

to learn what it is that everybody else apparently already knows (but won't tell), she again moved toward my ear. "People say that Frenchmen have sex almost at the drop of a hat *and* even if it's in the daytime!"

"Really," I answered, never before having realized that the Baptists placed a greater penalty on daytime sex. To some extent, I agree. I mean, who—who in their right mind would want to have sex in the daylight when your body can be looked at like just so much meat?

As interesting as Edna Louise's thoughts were, they were not nearly so memorable as some of Ruth's words from long ago. Maybe that's why now on the very eve of my departure Ruth began resting heavy on my mind. My heart told me to trust its judgment. It was right to see her, but the two blocks down to Nigger Bottoms would be laden with emotional obstacles. Maybe more than I could afford.

The first obstacle was leaving my room. Leaving the relative security of my own room to pass maybe within a few feet of one or both of my parents is not simple. Because to pass them is to automatically provoke them. But because I needed to see Ruth more than I needed to protect myself, I opened the door of my bedroom and walked quickly and quietly through our (thankfully) empty living room and out the front door.

The second obstacle, though, was not to be avoided. Mrs. Cora Jackson, who was sitting out on her front porch, called out as I passed by, "Where you going all alone on such a warm evening, Patty?"

"To the drugstore. I have this cough. Maybe a cold coming on."

"Drugstore's been closed for better'n an hour."

I felt like a caught criminal. "Oh, well," I laughed a meaningless laugh. "Maybe he'll be there. Doing something . . . "

Then as I resumed my walking, her voice caught up with me. "Patty, you mean to tell me that nobody has talked you out of your trip yet?"

Without slowing my step, I called back. "No, ma'am, nobody has."

Before Ruth saw me, I saw her just sitting out on her front porch trying to capture what puny little breezes there were with the help of a paper fan.

"Hello, Ruth," I said, walking up the three front steps to sit on an aged ladder-backed chair next to her.

"How you doing, Honey Babe?" she asked while smiling just enough to let me know how glad she was that I was there, but not enough to let me know how unusual she considered my coming.

Honey Babe? Honey Babe. It seemed such a long time since Ruth had called me that. Such a long time since I had been both little and worthy enough to deserve being called that. Hearing those words, sitting there on the porch, I knew exactly what I was there for. Nothing less than for the whole world to stop, back up, and let me be, at least for a little while, five or six again.

Little enough so it would be okay if she put her arms around me and big enough so I could understand what it was she was saying when she said, "No matter what it is that folks say, they ain't saying the truth when they say bad about you, Honey Babe. 'Cause you ain't bad. The good Lord knows . . . you ain't bad."

Lots of times I guess I've wanted to hear Ruth say that, but now with all the anguish this trip is causing my parents, I think I need to hear it. Why should I be ashamed of it? I've heard that Catholics of all ages stand in line for a little absolution. And aren't Baptists always dropping to their knees at the sight of salvation?

Maybe I can accept that. Say that I can. There's still one thing about my being here which isn't at all acceptable. Ignoring Ruth for all this time and now sneaking (yes, sneaking!) around here because of my selfishness . . . because of my need for her.

She gave herself quiet waves from her fully extended accordion-style fan. "Rain could sure do a heap of good for folks and their crops."

"I know," I said. "Everybody in town today has been complaining. Got a garden growing this year?"

"Claude planted tomatoes, okra, collards, and sweet corn and I planted the peonies, sweet Williams, and forget-me-nots."

"How come you're not growing gardenias? I remember you used to sometimes wear them pinned to your dress . . . always said they made the world smell sweet."

" 'Cause gardenias are perennials so they don't require no annual planting by me." Then Ruth looked me over closely and smiled. "You done got yourself one of the best memories I ever did see."

I laughed. "There's nothing very special about my memory. You just happen to like it 'cause it's your words that I tend to remember."

"That's sure enough right." Ruth laughed appreciatively as though it hadn't been her vanity, but somebody else's that had just been exposed. After a thoughtful silence, she spoke again. "I hears that you is soon going overseas."

"Guess everybody has heard that. My train leaves for New York tomorrow morning at a quarter to seven and on Thursday, I sail for France."

"Lord-dy! I hopes you finds what you has so long been looking for. I hopes the Bible makes good its promises."

"Its promises?"

"Why, right there in the Psalms where it says: 'Weeping may endure for a night, but joy . . . joy cometh in the morning.' "

I felt a rush of pain for the morning that had been so long in coming. And even more for the sorrows that had been so long in going. "Thank you for wishing me that. And you know, Ruth, that you have given me so much, and I . . . I have given you so little. And I wish that weren't true."

"Awl . . . I have cast my bread upon the waters and I have found it after many a day."

"What was it you found, Ruth?"

With one snap, the extended fan folded as compactly as a ruler and there on the spine of the fan, I was able to read the print: *Wiggins Funeral Home.*

"What I tried to give you," she said, "you done paid back with a heap more interest than they pay down at the Rice County Bank."

"Did I?" I asked, while already trying to commit myself to Ruth's more generous vision of me.

"As long as you live, Patty Babe, something of Ruth will live on too, 'cause, you know, that you is part me."

I found myself nodding in the twilight.

She went on talking and I was grateful that talk wasn't

required of me because I strongly suspected that my voice wasn't up to verbalizing.

"For a spell, even I didn't know how it was. Miz Bergen, I reckon she was the first to know. I knowed for sure she was the first to bring it to my attention. Once, long before you ever started to school, your ma was all fired up over some something you done did wrong and I tried to help you out. And that's when she said it to me. Looking straight at me, she said, 'Please stop thinking that you're the mother, Ruth, because you ain't. I'm the mother and you . . . you're only the maid.'

"'Reckon I don't never need no remind of that, Miz Bergen,' I told her, but truth is, I knowed that I did. After that, I tried doing for you only what I was paid to do. You ate good nourishing meals every day at the same hour. Your clothes were washed and ironed to a fare-thee-well, while I all the time told myself that this was the way it oughta be. Miz Bergen—she was right 'cause it ain't one bit natural to love somebody else's child as much as I loved you.

"Well, it wasn't much more'n a week, maybe two, later that something done come along to change all that. You came to the breakfast table looking for the world like you was going to continue your sleeping right there.

"Your pa looked up from his newspaper to say something to you—to this day I don't know what it was—but I heard your answer clear enough. It was, 'Uh uh . . . uh uh,' and with my own eyes, I seen him light out of his chair like his tail was afire to give you a whack across your face that was never meant for no child. No, sir! It was never meant for no child."

Her great mulatto head dropped against the back of her

wicker rocking chair and her eyes closed, more than closed. They seemed tightened as though resisting something as unrelenting as the direct rays of the sun. That's the way it seemed, only at this time there was no sun, only twilight.

For the first time, I noticed how much noise the squeaks and creaks of the floorboards made under the weight of her rocking chair, and the next thing I noticed was how very quiet everything really became as soon as Ruth gave up talking.

I began to wonder about her. At her age, this kind of talk coming at the end of a working day would wear an old lady out. Maybe that's why she stopped talking, so that I would whisper goodbye and then quickly and silently leave her be.

With her eyes closed, I allowed myself another more leisurely look at her face. The day's remaining light highlighted those rounded cheekbones and I thought now, as I have so often thought in the past, how very beautiful she is.

I stood up, reached down, and for a few moments touched the back of her hand. "Goodbye, Ruth," I said, thinking how that didn't even begin to express it. With all the reading I've done—the great poets, novelists, and three progressively difficult dictionaries—shouldn't I have something better than words so inadequate that they're barely worth the saying? Goodbye, Ruth. Pass the salt. How do you do. The grass is green. Inadequate!

She opened her eyes. I watched them register first surprise and then disappointment. "Sit for a spell longer, if you can spare the time."

I felt enormously pleased that she still wanted me and relieved that for at least a little while longer I didn't have to go back home, but could stay here in Nigger Bottoms with her. That's what I felt, but that wasn't anywhere near what I heard myself answer: "Well, I guess I could spare a little more time," I told her.

Once again I thought about the inadequacy of my words, and then it came to me that maybe my words were taking a bum rap. There's nothing wrong with my instrument—I use the language as well, probably better than most everybody else from around these parts. So the poets, the novelists, and maybe not even Noah Webster failed me.

I may have failed myself, though. I know there's a real inadequacy, but I don't think it's because I lack words, but because I lack courage. Enough courage to tell this old Negro woman that I love her.

Ruth had continued talking. Some of it I may have missed, but it had to do with that slap my father gave me and how, once he and my mother had left for the store, she found me missing.

"I looked for you high and I looked for you low. The house, the garage, the field. And every single place I could think to call, I'd call, asking if you'd done wandered down there and I had to listen to everybody tell me the same thing: We ain't seen no hide nor hair of Patty.

"Well, noontime came and noontime went and I had plum run out of places to look so I set myself down on the back steps and told myself that I ain't got no choice in this world, but to call your daddy. Looked like nothing less than a search party organized by the sheriff of the county was going to find you. Then it came into my head! The good Lord must have put it into my head that there was one last place needed looking.

"So fat old Ruth went around to the side of the house, bent down at that little wood door opening to the crawl space between the house and the bare ground and just a-called out, 'Honey Babe . . . oh, Honey Babe, is you is or is you ain't in there?'

"Well, sir, it was too dark for seeing and there was no-nothing for hearing, but just the same it was still growing in my head, growing stronger than ever that you was there. Just a-lying there on the hard dirt ground. So I sat down at the opening and began singing to the darkness, 'I looked over Jordan . . . And what did I see-e . . . A-coming for to car-ry me home . . .'

"Before long, I heard something, but I didn't stop, kept right on singing, 'A band of angels . . . Coming after me-e . . . Coming for to car-ry me home . . .'

"Then bless the Lord, I heard the scraping and then I saw you come crawling out on your elbows. And for the first time since I knowed you, you wasn't wearing nothing on your face. Looked to old Ruth like all those expressions you use to show had been slapped clear away.

"And so I sets you down on my lap and I commenced telling you what it was that I knowed to be true. Don't go feeling sorry for yourself, Honey Babe, thinking that you is some motherless child. 'Cause you ain't! You ain't never gonna be motherless 'cause you done gone and acquired . . . me!"

II · Europe

· 13 ·

As I WATCHED wave after sun-splashed wave break against the ship, I tried to find one that was an identical twin to another. Either my eyes couldn't capture the infinite variations or my memory couldn't record them. Probably both. Either way I knew, knew as clearly as if I'd been born to wave watching, that there never has been and never could be any such thing as one wave perfectly mirroring another.

The thought pleased me enormously. If grains of sand,

snowflakes, and ocean waves are allowed their differences, then why not people? Why not people! I wondered if my parents could have benefited from an extended period of ocean watching.

Could they have then come to my conclusion that because people are at least as different as ocean waves, their needs can't be satisfied with anything less than a custom job?

Here on this ship of strangers, I felt less like a stranger than I ever did on Main Street in Jenkinsville, Arkansas, or at Iris Glazer's not-quite-open open house back in Hein Park, Memphis, Tennessee, U.S.A.

And so all this air, sky, and endless water belonged to us all. I was no longer an intruder because I have finally found a place that is for more than Baptists only. Only five days from home, I was really beginning to believe what I had before only hoped was so: that this world is vast enough and varied enough for me to find "some little space that could become my space." But that phrase was stolen from Katherine Anne Porter.

Before the *Ryndam* left sight of the Statue of Liberty, the word was out that the novelist was occupying one of only six staterooms in first class. I was sharing the same sea air with the creator of *Flowering Judas* and *Pale Horse, Pale Rider*.

I envisioned dozens of circumstances which would practically compel Miss Porter to leave, at least for a little while, her first class accommodations for our more egalitarian tourist class.

Once while deck-walking early in the morning, I spotted a lady whose face showed such strength and beauty that I was convinced that it could belong to nobody else on this earth, but *her!* I reversed course and began following her, terrified that her immense perceptive apparatus would immediately signal to her what was happening. Yet, I couldn't not follow.

Her brown linen purse, which bore initials in fancy script, bounced from a shoulderstrap against her back. If I could get a little closer, I would be able to confirm the K.A.P. that had to be there. But the distance, the bounce, and the whimsical route of the letters made it difficult to be completely certain.

Then from a modest distance, a man in a deck chair also took note of her approaching figure and called, "Selma, did you bring my Coppertone?"

After that I decided that I was such an unreliable judge of what Miss Porter looks like that I might as well give up looking. Well, I didn't actually give up looking, but I did give up believing that my looking would succeed. Then, out of the blue, Arlene Hollander told me to scout up somebody to fill in for her at bridge that afternoon. "I'm going up to first class to hear Katherine Anne Porter."

"You are going to hear Katherine Anne Porter?"

"At two o'clock. She's going to read some of her poetry."

"And you got invited?"

Arlene looked at me with controlled amusement which I don't take as any great compliment. "Would I go otherwise?"

"Well, it just so happens that Katherine Anne Porter is currently my favorite writer—how did you get invited?" I asked, hoping that it wasn't dependent upon how many advanced degrees a person possessed. But it didn't matter what it depended upon because I was going too. And that's all there was to that!

With a presence commanding enough to make a West Pointer envious, Katherine Anne Porter looked at the twenty or so mostly young people who formed a crescent around her. "Anniversary in a Country Cemetery," she announced in a voice so clear that I knew I would remember it all my life.

> *This time of year, this year of all years, brought*
> *The homeless one home again;*
> *To the fallen house and the drowsing dust*
> *There to sit at the door*
> *Welcomed, homeless no more.*
> *Her dust remembers its dust*
> *And calls again*
> *Back to the fallen house this restless dust*
> *The shape of her pain*
> *This shape of her love*
> *Whose living dust reposes*
> *Beside her dust,*
> *Sweet as the dust of roses.*

After reading some more poems, some about Mexico and still others about love—or to be more specific, the loss of love—Miss Porter paused and with the last remnants of a Southern accent thanked us all.

The clapping which was loud and immediate was for the poems all right, but even more, I think it was for Miss Porter herself. Our way of collectively embracing her, as much for being art as for producing it.

That night I couldn't sleep, so I dressed by moonlight and went to the starboard deck. The wind was pure virgin wind, never once having had to spend itself against either outhouse or mountain range. And the prickling chill was great enough to send small shocks to my senses. But being here on this ship, my freshly energized senses told me, was exactly the right place to be.

I took a bent Viceroy from the pocket of my blouse and with more luck than skill was able to light it with the first match. Maybe if I could adequately explain it to my parents, they would come to appreciate all the things I've learned in these few days. The wonder of the individuality of an ocean wave, the art of Katherine Anne Porter, and the incredible fact of people who know a lot—people such as Michael Werner and Arlene Hollander—actually liking me. Me!

Ironically, the first "real" conversation that I had with Arlene almost ended our friendship. In the midst of my telling her that I can hardly believe my luck that a guy as handsome and bright as Michael would like me, Arlene twirled to gaze at me with unconcealed contempt.

"Have you looked in the mirror lately?"

"What!" It was my hair. My goddamn hair! It needed combing so badly that even my new friend found it imperative to inform me of my advanced state of dishevelment. I wanted to run away, but I felt suspended, frozen somewhere between fighting fury and disintegrating pain. I placed my finger inside my flexible watchband and twisted and twisted until the band snapped and my skin tore and then bled.

"Well, you really should take a careful look in the mirror," said the New Yorker, "because then you'd find out what everybody else knows. You're good looking. You tell amusing stories, and you listen to Michael with consummate interest."

The ship's library was quietly lit in a way that was completely compatible with the hour of 4:15 in the morning. By ten minutes after five, there were nine sheets of Holland-America stationery folded into an envelope that was addressed to Mr. & Mrs. Harry Bergen, Jenkinsville, Arkansas, U.S.A.

Just before bringing the flap to my tongue, I removed the pages for a final reading. I think—I felt—I had almost certainly written what I had set out to write. A letter so clean with clarity that it would be totally impossible for them not to understand it . . . for them not to understand me.

It was that thought that I carried with me as I tiptoed back into my stateroom and fell, fully clothed, across my bed. And now waiting for me was just that quality of sleep that comes only to the very deserving.

I woke to the glockenspiel. I had slept through breakfast and now the ship's steward was glockenspieling out the ten o'clock call for broth and crackers. It's supposed to hold us passengers until twelve when a four-course lunch is served, but after the breakfasts the Dutch serve up, who needs to be held?

I headed toward the aft deck, not so much for the chicken broth as for Michael, who would never willingly be separated from food freely given. It's not that I blame him—I mean he's about as thin as a guy can be and still be healthy. It's just that once he returns to his *pension* in Zurich, then the meals become decidedly skimpy. The American students returning to Swiss medical schools are forever discussing ways to supplement their guest-house cuisine.

"And where the hell have you been hiding?" I twirled to look at the slight-chip-on-the-shoulder good looks of Michael Joseph Werner. He took a sip from the broth-filled white mug without even momentarily removing his head-on stare from my face.

"Oh, well, I'm really sorry, Michael. I guess I just slept through breakfast," I said, grateful that Arlene wasn't around to hear my apology. On the first day out, she asked me why I allowed Michael, a virtual stranger, to push me around.

Right off, I told her that Michael didn't push me around— at least not very much. I tried to explain that while I didn't exactly love Michael's temper, it did seem familiar. It was as though he understood me now, had understood me for a long time. But as soon as that came out of my mouth, I knew I had stumbled into something dumb. So I tried to get out of it by saying that there's something very natural about his anger toward me.

But Arlene kept looking at me with an eye so skeptical that she must have spent years perfecting it.

"For God's sake," I told her, feeling myself pinched into the corner. "Can't you see that that's exactly the way that men are supposed to treat women?"

I leaned back against the railing, close enough to let my arm whisper against Michael's. Within moments, he seemed soothed. "At least," he said, breaking into a modest laugh, "you didn't have to dress for dinner."

I laughed too although the joke was very definitely on me. "Please excuse me. I have to dress for dinner," were the exact words that I had used. It was the first morning Arlene, Howie, Michael, and I were in the salon playing bridge.

Actually, they were playing bridge while tutoring me in the fine art of destroying your enemies with trumps, tricks, and finesses. I was pleased, flattered even, that these smart and handsome people would bother with me.

Arlene, for example, is only three years older than me and she's already working on her master's degree in French renaissance literature. Of course, Michael and Howie are both very smart too, but you sort of expect that from guys who are Jewish.

Anyway, I was taking my bridge instruction on that first morning pretty well when the ship must have hit the biggest single wave in the Atlantic, because the *Ryndam* crunched forward, crunched backward, crunched forward. Then it was calm again—the ship, not my stomach. Immediately I knew that I had an old and familiar race to win, but I didn't say that.

Instead I just stood up and with what Michael was later to describe as "stage presence" announced, "Please excuse me. I have to dress for dinner."

Well, probably nobody would ever have known any different if Michael hadn't, for some still unexplained reason, taken it into his head to watch me from the porthole.

And now that phrase (spoken with exaggerated elegance) seems to be known by just about everybody on board the *Ryndam* as the expression to use when you're on the verge of upchuking your fool head off, but wish to do so with style.

Actually Michael goes even further by assuring me that I have made a contribution for all time, not only to maritime vocabulary, but also to the international folklore of the sea.

$\cdot 14 \cdot$

THE CAPTAIN'S FAREWELL dance was billed as the final and single most important event of the voyage. The Grande Salon, for example, had been closed to passengers since noon because the decorations were supposed to be both special and surprising.

The very first surprise was Michael himself, whose usual well-scrubbed scruffiness gave way to a well-ordered handsomeness. I wondered how much of it came from his blue shirt and tan suit. The pants actually matched the jacket. And how much from the fact that for the first time since I've known him, his hair wasn't falling defiantly across his forehead.

As we walked along the deck toward the Grande Salon, I told him that he looked very nice. He led me over to the railing. The lights from the deck spilled over the water and made wave watching a real possibility, but I knew Michael well enough to know that gazing at waves rather than into his dark and assertive eyes would kindle his well-exercised temper.

Then for the first time it occurred to me that looking away from this man was not about to happen anyway, for Michael's face was beginning to fill me with the most intense kind of pleasure.

He struck a pose so casual that I knew it wasn't casual at all. "Well, when are you coming to Zurich?"

"Well," I repeated, playing for a moment of time. I was pleased and surprised that he liked me well enough to want to see me again. But why should that surprise me? Hadn't he spent practically every waking moment with me? And wouldn't I expect Howie to invite Arlene Hollander to visit him? Yes, yes, yes, but that doesn't make it any the less surprising that Michael Joseph Werner could actually find something likable about me!

"Well . . . " I said, again, deciding that I had to strike that word from my vocabulary once and for all, "if you really want me to, Michael, I think that I could." At the same time trying to estimate the distance between Göttingen and Zurich.

This time he kissed me nicely. Not like all those other

times when he tried to hungrily stuff himself with kisses in the same indiscriminate way he's always stuffing himself with food. For the last six days, I've been wondering what's wrong with me. Why was I so secretly grateful that he shared his stateroom with three males while I shared mine with three females? But now in the sharing of this particular kiss, I forgot to be grateful.

And so the fact that I had never felt a romantic thing for either Marshall Lubin or the Jenkinsville farmboys didn't prove anything!

We moved away from the railing, away from the cold, persistent ocean spray. Then Michael looked at me as though he had suddenly come upon answers to questions never asked. "You've caught yourself a doctor," he said, with obvious satisfaction.

At the same moment, I felt both an enormously positive and an enormously negative charge. I didn't know which one to react to. Positive? Negative? Neither? Both?

"I think you know that I like you, Michael . . . a lot. I think you're very intelligent and witty, and I even think you're good looking, but . . . but please don't make it out that I've captured you."

Michael looked at me as though I had with malice aforethought let all the air from his balloons, ordered rain on his birthday, and wished him a mouthful of cavities. "It's only an expression, for Christ's sake!"

"I know, I know it is, but I still don't like what it expresses."

"Oh, for Christ's sake, if you hadn't lived all your life in the sticks, then you'd know that it was only an expression!"

"That phrase isn't so original that it's unknown in

Arkansas. Actually it may be just as popular in Jenkinsville as it is in Forest Hills, but I still don't happen to like it." He had turned his head from me. "Oh, Michael," I said, moving to face him, "please don't turn away from me now. Ever since we've met you've felt comfortable telling me what you didn't like about me—my gazing off in the distance when you speak to me, my swimsuit which you claimed was manufactured for the varicose set—and I could go on . . . "

Michael's face had set. "And I told you that it was only an expression! And this is the dumbest conversation I've ever had!"

I could scream because he was choosing not to hear me. "Whatever it is, it's not dumb. If we belong together, Michael, it's because we each have something to give. Not just you giving and me taking, I'd hate that, but both of us giving, taking. I want you to understand that I need to have value too!"

"All right! All right! I tracked you down. I captured you. Are you satisfied? Now, for God's sake, I'd like to go! The music is getting cold."

Is that what he thinks this is all about? Who's tracked whom down? Suddenly he was pulling me toward the Grande Salon with as much gentleness as a bulldozer moving an enormous earth-embedded boulder. But I didn't resist. There was no need to. Because the really important thing was that I didn't know any way to make him understand what he preferred not knowing.

· 15 ·

AT GARE ST. LAZARE, Arlene and I were among the first passengers off the boat train, and considering the bulk and weight of our luggage, we climbed up the stairs with surprising speed to rush from the open doors into the late afternoon of a Paris day.

From the very top step of the massive station, I took my first real look at the street scene below. What I saw threw my senses into a dance of frenzied greed, and I knew that

I had to find a way to become a part of it. Couldn't waste time. Had to belong to it all. And I had to belong to it now!

I wanted to ride to Montparnasse on the rear platform of that passing bus; wanted to stroll the wide boulevards hand-in-hand with some new boy I was beginning to love. And within the same measure of time and space, I wanted to drink espresso and eat decadent desserts at that little side-walk café across the way; then, on some irrepressible whim, I'd buy myself an extravagant silk scarf from a shop so far off the beaten track that it had never before been discovered by a mere tourist.

I had to experience all those things and a thousand more while simultaneously exploring every single street, searching out every face to find one that might be willing to teach me all those things that I was born needing to know.

Yet for all the freshness and all the wonder of Paris, this was not the first time that my senses had exploded while trying to capture the dazzling beauty and enchantment within this world. Somewhere, someplace, it had happened to me before. Had to have happened because it felt too real to have been only a dream.

Yes, yes, that was it! But such a long time ago. I was only seven—certainly no more than eight. And one star-filled night, I was riding the great Ferris wheel high above the Memphis Cotton Carnival when, for at least a moment, my gently swaying gondola paused at the very top.

Arlene instructed (in apparently faultless French) a mischievous-eyed taxi driver to take her to the Cité Universitaire and me to the Hotel Vaucluse. As soon as he drove off, I understood why he kept a crucifix dangling from the dashboard of his Renault. He wasn't taking fares across Paris; he was competing in the Indianapolis 500.

I guess I minded a lot because I had paid such a big price for the privilege of being here on this continent. I deserved to see it with more clarity than through the blurred side window of a racing car.

Then Arlene objected to the wind blowing from my completely lowered window. For moments I pretended not to have heard her, but then my selfishness became a barrier to the full enjoyment of this city. So I grudgingly raised my window by a few, very careful inches.

Much too quickly, the cab came to a cops-and-robbers stop and the polo-shirted driver announced, "Voilà, mam'-selles, Cité Universitaire." Arlene then explained to him in French what she had twice previously explained to me in English. That the cab was to wait for her, since she was arriving a day ahead of schedule and wanted to make certain that her room was now available.

After she disappeared behind a pale stucco wall made beautiful by a network of sun and leaf shadow, I silently called upon the God of my fathers.

Listen to me, God. I know. I know I'm a nudge. I bother you only when I need something (and, God knows, that's often enough), but maybe if you think I deserve it you'll help me now.

That's when my concentration was broken by the driver, who turned around to speak to me. One word sounded like *roses,* but I'm not really sure of that. "I'm sorry, sir," I admitted, "but I don't speak French."

He nodded and smiled as though he wished me luck, or maybe he was indicating that I was going to need luck. I couldn't be sure. At any rate, he had broken more than my concentration; he had gotten me out of my God-nudging mood. Just as well, because if there's a God up there who's listening in, I really can't imagine him involving himself in something as shabby as helping me out while hurting Arlene. But it wouldn't be hurting Arlene. Maybe inconveniencing her, but that's all. Why is it such a big deal if she stays with me tonight, just for a single night?

I mean, I think it would be scary for anyone, being alone in a strange country without even knowing the words for food or water.

When I saw her reappear, I knew that the good Lord had not only heard my plea, but had actually joined with me in my conspiracy, for Arlene wore an expression of "This world is so dumb that it doesn't deserve to have me in it." Hallelujah! And thank you, God, for sealing Arlene from her room tonight with a sticky bit of your celestial red tape. Surely by tomorrow, I'd be infinitely more adept at facing Paris alone.

"Oh, too bad," I offered. "Aren't they letting you have your room tonight?" I sounded so obviously hypocritical that anyone even half as smart as this candidate for a master's degree would pick it up in less time than it would take light to travel across a country lane.

Arlene looked surprised. "Oh, I have the room. It's only that the concièrge has the key and he's not expected back for at least an hour."

"Wonderful, Arlene," I said with a little too much badly manufactured enthusiasm. "Makes it so much more convenient than having to sleep elsewhere for the night."

She gave me 375 francs for her share of the taxi ride.

"Three hundred and seventy-five francs," I asked incredulously, "for only half of a taxi ride?"

"Francs, not dollars," explained Arlene. "One thousand francs equals three dollars . . . remember?"

I nodded. "Oh, yes! Sure. Sorry."

"Well . . . " she said. "I wish you all kinds of luck and don't forget what I told you on the *Ryndam*."

"Oh . . . " I said, purposely vague, hoping that that would inspire her to repeat it. Twice on ship she had given me detailed instructions on "getting structured in a foreign country," and I had loved it . . . loved it far beyond the words of advice which in themselves were useful enough. What it was, I think, was this girl, three years older and maybe six years more competent actually bothering with me . . . bothering to give me something.

"First thing tomorrow," she was saying, "go over to Boulevard Raspail, to the Alliance Française and sign up for their beginning French class."

"Beginning French class," I repeated.

Arlene nodded her approval as though I was already a student and learning well. "Then cross Raspail and go directly over to Montparnasse—it's only an eight- or ten-block walk. Pass Montparnasse and from that point, ask anybody to direct you to the American Club."

"Avenue Montparnasse. The American Club."

Arlene smiled as though she was already the esteemed professor that she would someday be and I was her most gifted student. "I'm very glad we met," she said, letting her smile linger on. "You're the first person I've ever known who hailed from Jenkinsville, Arkansas."

The farther I go from my home town, the more humor

people seem to discover in its name. "It's okay—until I met you and Michael, I had never known anybody from New York City." I was afraid that my large effort at making small talk was tiring Arlene. She had a lot of really important things to do and I didn't want to impede her or have her think I was a bore. But most of all, I didn't want her to even begin to suspect that I was afraid to be alone.

This conversation had to be immediately terminated, and terminated by me while I could still appear strong and competent. I wanted her to see that I was really tough, and because of that toughness I didn't need her or anybody. I could manage very well alone, thank you. "Well, Arlene," I said, holding out my hand, "I hope it'll be a good year for you; I know your thesis will go well."

She shook my hand for a moment and then for a still longer moment, she merely held it. "Call me when you get settled. You know how to reach me."

"Yes," I said, jumping at the invitation. "Yes, I surely do." Suddenly two diverse—maybe not totally diverse—thoughts struck me! Arlene Hollander with all her master's degree competence was also more than a little frightened and secondly, strangeness of strangenesses, I think she likes me.

That she had been very friendly on board ship was undeniable, but I had, for the most part, considered it nothing more than a courtesy to her boyfriend's best friend, Michael Werner. But now that Michael and Howie are both en route to Zurich, there's no reason to continue extending the courtesy unless . . . unless she actually does like me.

I threw my arms around her and hers like a reflex tightened around me. Then just as suddenly and without so much as a "So long, Arlene," I quickly re-entered the cab and

directed my now tightly stretched voice toward the driver.
"Hotel Vaucluse on Rue Pierre Nicol."

Then I began to explore seriously this dumbness of mine.
How can I so consistently dismiss every single item of evidence which indicates that there just might be people in this
world who happen to like me? Michael wants to marry me,
Arlene wants to be my friend, so I couldn't possibly be doing
everything wrong. Then why don't I know that? Why can't
I really know that?

As I tried to supply the answer to my own question, I
saw rows of pastel buildings wearing ornate wrought-iron
balconies and, at the same time that I was seeing this elegant
French city, I was also "seeing" a drab American town.

Jenkinsville, Arkansas. An early September morning in
1938. I wake with a Christmas-morning kind of excitement
even though I've been sleeping for too long in my own
sweat. Jenkinsville has been suffering through a late summer's heat wave and this would be just another damp rot
day except for one thing. I am six years old and today is my
first day of school.

Next to my bed is the red-and-blue plaid book satchel.
Opening it, I smell the newness of my primary tablet; I
slide open the pristine pencilbox which came with two
finely sharpened yellow pencils, one virgin gum eraser, a
red pocket pencil sharpener, and a strange instrument with
an ice-pick point that makes perfect circles.

After breakfast my mother comes into my room. I think
she is going to tell me that I should be leaving now, but she
doesn't. What she wants is to fix my hair. Her way. But I
won't allow it because it's already fixed my way. So I take
my prize book satchel and run out the door. And just as I

am beginning to believe in the safety of the public sidewalks, she calls after me.

"Don't expect any of the first graders to like you, Patricia Ann, 'cause they won't! And don't expect Miss Blackwell to like you either, 'cause she won't! They're all going to take one look at the plain way you've combed your hair and they're not going to like you! Not a single one of them is ever going to like you!"

Inside the tightness of my fist something was pressing uncomfortably against my palm. I opened my hand to find Arlene Hollander's bills.

As I watched the taxi travel a boulevard shaded on both sides by aging chestnut trees, I closed my eyes. Even so, it felt as though Arlene and the not-to-be-seen Paris sun were making me a present of their warmth.

· 16 ·

As THEY MOVED with an almost mechanical gait toward me, the growing crescent of my townspeople chanted, "Jew Nazi lover . . . Jew Nazi lover . . . Jew Nazi lover." I moved away while calling back to them, explaining that really Anton was never, NEVER in his whole life a Nazi! Only a not-very-brave man who was too decent to kill and too scared to die for the fatherland.

But it wasn't until now, now when I could see the tightness of their lips—"Jew Nazi lover! Jew Nazi lover! Jew Nazi lover!"—and the narrowing of their eyes that I came to understand that I was soon to die because not even one of them would ever allow himself to listen. And I was going to die in a way that nobody would ever describe as merciful.

When the crescent moved to encircle, I felt a damp, astringent blast from their collective breaths as they shouted with an absolute on-the-beat precision, "JEW NAZI LOVER! JEW NAZI LOVER! JEW NAZI LOVER!"

My eyes jerked open to gaze upon the Hotel Vaucluse's paint-is-a-peeling ceiling and older-than-thou wallpaper featuring tiny garlands of no longer fresh pink flowers strung together with whimsical blue ribbons.

"Nobody's going to hurt me," I whispered to my rapidly beating heart. "I'm not there . . . there in Jenkinsville anymore. I'm here. Here safe in Paris, France."

But all of my bad dream wasn't only a dream because outside on the street there was real commotion, real chanting going on: "Legumes du jardin . . . bon marché! Legumes du jardin . . . bon marché!"

Slowly shifting my reclining body into a sitting position on this strange, soft-as-a-pillow mattress, I looked at my watch. Only quarter to six. Morning had been a long time coming, but still I felt comforted that I had, in some fashion, made it through the night.

I spread the curtains apart and threw open the almost floor-to-ceiling French-windows to look out upon a day that hadn't as yet been completely lit by the sun.

Two stories below, a triangle of intersecting streets was coming alive with open-air stalls and pushcarts being loaded with small mountains of primary-colored fruits and vegetables. Practically all of them were roofed by a slant of weather-worn tarpaulin, but here and there a fringed bi-colored beach umbrella crowned the enterprise.

A street smell of incredible sweetness wafted up. Cantaloupe! I searched the marketplace to match the olfactory with the visual, but the closest I could come to matching was a barechested man unloading boxes of bananas from a battered farm truck.

As I systematically searched the mounds of produce for those elusive melons, my eyes stalled on a row of white rabbits and a single dun-colored lamb dangling in eternal serenity on outdoor hooks in front of the store-front sign "Boucherie."

Then close, but unseen, cathedral bells began ringing so celestially that my first thought was that something momentous must have happened. A pope had died? Or been born? But my second thought was to check my watch. Precisely six o'clock. Nothing even semi-momentous about that.

The blue haze of morning was slowly being replaced by pale yellow sunshine, but because it emanated from the earth's edge, the carts and even the people seemed to throw especially long and searching shadows.

There were perceptibly more people now—mostly women wearing Cuban heels and carrying net or cloth shopping bags in their hands, who began moving around and about the stalls and carts of the marketplace. "Legumes du jardin . . . bon marché . . . legumes du jardin . . . bon marché!"

When the soles of my still bare feet felt as though they were being impaled on the warped wooden floor slats, I sat down on my narrow wrought-iron balcony to watch a heavy-bodied woman wearing a lavender smock wash windows opening out to her own third floor balcony.

I wondered how many queens in how many kingdoms ever had such a front row center seat upon their world.

There was knocking at my door. Automatically I called out, "Who is it?" before I remembered the perfectly obvious. Neither the Hotel Vaucluse lady—here they call her the concièrge—nor her husband seems to understand a single word of English.

The door opened. From the keyhole, Madame Lucier pulled out a brass key connected to a long brass chain that terminated at a diaper pin attached to her more than ample waistband.

"Bonjour, mam'selle," she sang out with a kind of all embracing cheerfulness. "Voilà, votre petit déjeuner."

"Bonjour, madame. Merci," I answered while thinking at least two almost simultaneous things. First, I had just given forth with two sentences comprising three words which were roughly fifty percent of my entire French vocabulary. And second, exactly how silly did I look sitting here on this iron balcony in my nightgown?

Madame's work, though, seemed to have equipped her not only with simple efficiency, but also with exemplary discretion, for she gave not even a hint that one of her guests might have possibly strayed beyond acceptable limits.

She went right on with her job of setting out my breakfast. There were two obviously hot pitchers, a cup and saucer rimmed with chrysanthemums, and a plate rimmed with violets on which there were two crescent moons of flaky bread, two curls of what looked like butter, and a small crystal dish filled with what had to be marmalade.

As I tried to come up with something in English that I could translate into my minimal French, something that might salvage a bit of dignity lost, she turned and headed toward the door while calling out, "Bon appetit, mam'selle."

"Au revoir, madame, and merci a lot."

As soon as the door closed behind her, I put on a blue circular skirt and a white blouse with an open collar and forgot all about my dignity, but I did wonder what possible combination of words I had used with Madame yesterday to give her the impression that I wanted breakfast. And room serviced, no less!

From my father, I had once heard about room service—how expensive and all it is. Once when he was at the Chase Hotel in St. Louis on one of his semi-annual buying trips, he decided to "save a little time," so he ordered up a couple of scrambled eggs, bacon, toast, and coffee and for that he had to pay a buck sixty-five. And that didn't even include the tip!

Well, I guess it's like what the folks back home say. "Them that dances got to pay the fiddler." Guess it's the same for those who eat via room service except it's Madame la Concièrge that must be paid. I told myself that at least I wouldn't allow room service prices (no matter how high) to interfere with my ability to enjoy my breakfast. Just the opposite!

I slid the little round table over to my window-on-the world, clasped the warm pitcher of milk with one hand and the even hotter pitcher of coffee (as dark as the very richest earth of the Arkansas deltalands) with the other. And rising on that steam (breathe in deeply, take it all in) was the undiluted aroma of coffee strong and pure.

Without having yet tasted it, I knew that it was nothing like what old Mr. Joe C. Thomas (everybody back home calls him Mr. Josie) pours from his big round urn down at the Victory Cafe. And the Vaucluse brew was even further removed from that powdery instant stuff that my mother spoons into her cup.

I poured part coffee and part hot milk into my cup, stirred, and took a long thoughtful drink. It wasn't bitter and yet at this incredible strength it could have easily become so. A minute more brewing or a second reheating.

After only one sip, I wasn't even completely certain that I liked it—yet I could never easily forget it.

Maybe it was because, in a way, this coffee reminds me of something. Maybe . . . maybe only a philosopher or a mad man would make this connection, but it's a little like life. I mean it's powerful going down and that doesn't even take into account the aftertaste, which really takes getting used to.

· 17 ·

JUST INSIDE the baronial front doors of the Alliance Française was the office of le Directeur. A woman of middle years, wearing what back home is referred to as a "porch" dress (too good to do housework in, not really good enough to go to town in, but just about the right thing to wear when you're sitting out catching the evening breezes), was cutting stencils in the smallish outer office of le Directeur.

"Bonjour, madame."

"Bonjour, mademoiselle."

I felt as though I must be the only person in France who couldn't speak the language. ". . . Well, uh." And help-lessly presumptuous, for I had no right to expect her to un-derstand my language. "I would like to enroll in your beginning French class."

"Mais oui, mademoiselle, à dix heures pour les debutants. Lundi et mercredi."

"Well, you see, I don't speak at all. Not even a little bit."

"Je comprends," she said, handing me an application blank that looked as though it had been cut from one of her stencils.

And with a little understanding and a little more guess-work, I began filling in the blanks:

NOM ET PRÉNOMS: *PATRICIA ANN BERGEN*
ÂGE: *18*
ADRESSE À PARIS: *VAUCLUSE HOTEL-7 RUE PIERRE NICOL*
DATE D'ARRIVÉE EN FRANCE: *SEPTEMBER 22, 1950*
NATIONALITÉ: *AMERICAN*
NIVEAU DE FRANÇAIS:
    DEBUT: *X*
    INTERMÉDIAIRE: _____
    AVANCÉ: _____

When she finally looked up from her stencil, I smiled while handing over my application. She accepted it (along with five thousand francs) and gave me a schedule and a Carte d'Étudiant, but not once within our multiminuted exchange did she ever return my smile. Well, let her keep it. Good luck to her!

If only I could have spoken French for a minute, I'd have

used my ability to remind Madame la Stencil Cutter that without people like me, she'd have nobody to cut stencils for.

Also, I'd get the fact across that if she has to feel contempt for my ignorance then she should, at the very least, temper it with the demonstrable fact that I'm now trying to overcome this deficiency. Shouldn't I get a little credit for that?

Then as I approached the door, I heard her call after me, "Au revoir, mademoiselle." But as I turned to overenthusiastically respond, she was already back at work on her stencil, so in my best-sounding French, I told her goodbye too.

The very next moment I get some free thinking time, I'm going to sit right down and try once and for all to figure it out. I mean, why is it I'm always so quick to believe that people are thinking . . . believing the worst about me?

As I walked back down the corridor, I passed two women who seemed to be sharing something special in their adoptive tongue. One wore a wind-taunting sari while her friend was wearing a colorfully striped caftan that couldn't have come from anyplace but Africa.

Then suddenly their heads dropped backward and the women were laughing. That laugh—was it shared French laughter, or did they each unbeknownst to the other find their timbre and pitch by returning to their ancestral tongues?

But just as soon as the question was posed, I understood where and how I erred, and why it is that a laugh, like a cry, doesn't ever need translation.

I fingered my pale green student identification card while experiencing an emotion that seemed fresh, at least to me. I felt pride . . . pride at being accepted here. Did I need to remind myself that it's one of life's few certainties that nobody with five thousand francs had ever been turned away by Madame la Stencil Cutter?

No, I didn't need a reminder and yet the pride never budged because I could never forget that the real getting here hadn't been easy. Not easy at all.

I felt my eyes blur with what are called "tears of happiness." That's what they may call them, but that's not what they are—not really! Because even if there is now a view of happiness before me, I can only see it through eyes long conditioned by pain.

Can't I even now congratulate myself? I have reached the first part of a difficult objective. So why can't I just focus on that instead of standing here in the middle of an empty corridor with my "tears of happiness" flowing as unrelentingly as flood water? Because the joy of accomplishment is not all that I'm feeling.

I'm also feeling the price I have paid to get here. *"V'yis-gadal . . . Yisgadal . . . "* Is my father really reciting the prayers of the dead for me?

Let him, let him, let him! What do I care about his losses? I can't help him. I wish I could help him with his, but I can't even help me with mine.

With my father—with both of my parents—I had experienced our separation long before this sitting *shiva* thing. Who knows, maybe at one time they really did like me . . . but I don't remember that.

The only real difference is that my father has now made the loss official and so I can no longer pretend that things aren't all that bad. That this is only a temporary phase that we're all just plodding through. Losing my pretend, is that what I'm really crying about?

Well, it's not the only thing. There's you, Anton. You who began the process that made me realize that my world could be vaster and more varied than that tiny town in the northeast corner of Arkansas. And it certainly wasn't I, Anton, who preached the glorious doctrine of "feelings are good for sharing."

Well, I've been a really great practitioner of your teachings. Boy, you could hardly find a better practitioner than me! And now maybe it's time that you listened: because for all my struggle, I'm not sure what I've gained. Or if my life is better for all you've taught me. I'm smarter all right and my vision is sharper, but still sometimes I think, so what is that to me?

Seeing, knowing, feeling are things that have to be paid for. How come you never told me . . . how come you never even hinted at the expense? And please tell me why I can't ever seem to find my way back to pretend?

But don't go thinking that I'm critical of you, Anton, because really I'm not. Not a bit! It's just that you're not here. I'm alone and I'm frightened and you're not here. And you're not ever going to be here for me.

I'm sorry to say this, but I don't believe you should run around starting projects that you're not going to finish. It's not fair to go around abandoning things . . . abandoning people. Telling me what a great person—a person of value— I am. You told me that, remember? Just before you left to go get yourself killed. And I begged you not to go, but you knew too much to listen to me.

Then I asked you to take me with you, to please, please, just take me with you, but still you wouldn't listen! I guess the problem was I had no way to convince you of something that I already understood: I would have never permitted your death. Even with the FBI's bullets tearing through your head, I don't think you would have died because I would have held you so closely that you could never have slipped off.

Don't you understand? Even now? That for as long as I lived, I would have been like a massive anchor, firmly securing you to this earth.

·18·

"Pardon, mademoiselle, you need assistance?"

"What?"

"You have been standing on that spot for some while. I thought you might need some help? Directions? Information?"

"Oh, well, no thanks," I said, sneaking my first real look at his face which was a young face, only a shade above or below the twenty-five-year mark. It struck me—maybe it was only because he was smiling a teasing, yet honest smile—that here at last was a face that hid few secrets.

"I was just standing here," I answered, already wishing I could erase that remark, "because I've already found the director's office."

He introduced himself with a smoothness that bypassed my awkwardness. His name was Roger David Auberon and he taught two French classes a week at the Alliance Française. "And you," he asked, "tell me what is your name and what are you doing so far from the states?"

"I came to explore your beautiful city. My name is Patty Bergen and—and you knew I was an American," I said, allowing it to dawn upon me that he had addressed me in English. "You knew that before I had ever said a word."

"Naturally."

"How?"

"Easy."

"Yes, but how?"

"Well, Africans look like Africans, Frenchmen resemble Frenchmen, and Americans appear remarkably like—"

"Americans," I said in conjunction with Roger Auberon. Then together we laughed, as together we had already walked out the front door of the Alliance Française.

"Also," he said, "it helps if you have a good eye and . . . I have a good eye."

"Do you?" I asked, not because I doubted it for a moment, but because I hoped that my response would encourage him to elaborate. And it did.

"But of course. Chefs have good noses, musicians good ears, and photographers—I'm a photographer—have to possess the good eye. N'est-ce pas?"

"Yes, but I thought—you just finished telling me that you were a teacher here at the Alliance Française."

"But how else can I afford my darkroom supplies? Film for my camera? Rent? Bread? A glass or two of *vin ordinaire*?"

"You mean to tell me that you don't charge your customers?"

He breathed in deep and that breath seemed to elongate his thin body. Even so, he wasn't very tall. Not more than three or four inches taller than me. Maybe five feet seven or eight at the most. "You think I'm a mere commercial taker of pictures? Smile! Snap! Five hundred francs, please."

"No, I know you're not," I said, also knowing that I had pretty quickly caught on to something about him. "Your camera is only the instrument through which you express your art." I had thought that that sounded extraordinarily intelligent when I had first read that comment of Henri Cartier-Bresson's in a recent issue of *Reader's Digest*.

Suddenly Roger grabbed my hand as though I had just rounded home plate. "Absolutely so!" he said, as he went on talking, explaining, really, with fluid animation about the photographer's need to communicate "his vision." I found it inordinately difficult to understand exactly what it was he was saying.

Something about the way he held my hand seemed to interfere with the normal flow of oxygen to my brain. And if that wasn't bad enough, another pretty awful thing began happening. My palms were now oozing sweat. Without much success, I tried picturing Ginger Rogers or even Betty Hutton with clammy paws. And then I began wondering if that constituted a fatal flaw, I mean fatal to ever being loved.

After a long walk, we turned a corner onto a leafy boulevard and Roger pointed to a sidewalk café. "That's where we're going," he said, letting me in on the information that we were actually heading somewhere together. "The Café aux Deux Magots is where your famous American writer, Ernest Hemingway, once spent his afternoons."

"Really?" I asked, feeling extraordinarily privileged. "Ernest Hemingway happens to be one of my all-time favorites."

Roger found a sidewalk table with just the right amount of shade, view, and privacy. "And who are your other favorites?" He asked as though after great French photographers, there was nothing that he liked to discuss quite so much as great American writers.

"Well . . . " I wondered if I knew him well enough to confess this. "Well, I know he's great and everything and I know the critics love him more than anybody else, but I don't. And the funny thing is, I've tried. Really I have!"

I could tell that he was growing increasingly disoriented. I can appreciate that. One of my bad habits is that sometimes when I'm working my hardest to explain something, I find that I'm off on some improbable tangent which does more to muddify than to clarify. Someday I've just got to correct that.

Anyway, I decided that there was nothing left for me to do but to make a clean uncomplicated statement. And if he thinks I'm a literary barbarian, well, I'm going to come right out and tell him to place it on the record that I'm no hypocritical literary barbarian. "The truth is William Faulkner is not one of my favorites. I mean, you see, he bores me."

"I read *The Sound and the Fury* when I went to school in Atlanta—no, I was already back in France."

"Atlanta, Georgia? What were you doing there?"

"Papa took us to Atlanta when I was three years old. He was chef at Atlanta's only French restaurant."

"Did he—did you all like it there?"

Roger smiled, a little guiltily I thought, as though he might be positioning himself somewhere between truth and tact. "Well," he shrugged, "we all had our complaints."

"Tell me what they were," I said, anxious to hear my country's faults taken out, examined, and catalogued just like any other defective commodity. Maybe what I really wanted was somebody else's more objective finding on just why it is that I've never felt all that much at home in my own homeland.

"Papa's complaint was with the Americans' undeveloped palate. Mama never adjusted to America. She missed her family and friends too much. But we lived close enough to the Eliot playground for my sister Suzanne and I to generally enjoy ourselves. I suppose, though, that the greatest disappointment was Papa's. He never made enough money to triumphantly return to France to open his own restaurant."

I must have said, "Oh," in a flat-sounding way that indicated to him that I didn't consider Chef Auberon's inability to open his own restaurant a tragedy of truly epic proportions, because Roger simply shrugged as though passing both me and my comment off. "Obviously, you do not understand the French temperament."

"Well, I just got here," I said, in a way calculated to convey the thought that understanding a country that pre-dates Christ would take even me a couple of days.

"To the French, winning—*le triomphe*—is everything!"

"You think only to the French?" I interjected. "You've

158

never seen the Jenkinsville, Arkansas, football team play against our arch rival, the Wynne City Wildcats. Talk about winning being everything. Boy, it's everything and then some!"

"Maybe," said Roger, obviously not convinced. "But, you see, only the French have the imagination to believe in victories never achieved."

He had to be kidding or at least speaking philosophically because nobody unless they were born loons could believe something like what he said. Something that's never been. "You don't mean . . . really?"

"As you walk around this city, read the statues."

"Read the statues?"

"Every third statue in Paris depicts a noble France conquering her enemies."

"So?"

"So when do you suppose France last conquered an enemy?"

I tried conjuring up old history lessons. French and Indian Wars. Recurrent battles between the French and the English. But who was the victor and who was the vanquished? Damn! I knew I should have paid more attention in class. You never can tell when something might turn out to be important. "I can't remember, not exactly."

"Neither can anybody else now alive because we have to return a century to Napoleon for our battles won and even he had the rather colossal misfortune to lose it all at Waterloo."

"And you mean to sit there and tell me that the French newspapers haven't as yet got around to reporting that bit of information?"

Roger lifted his shoulders while pressing his lower lip outward. "Oh, they reported it, but some of us still don't wish to believe it."

"Don't believe what you know?"

"We don't wish to believe what we know. It interferes with our need to believe in our own glory, in all the glory that is France! Come," he said, twirling his head toward the waiter, "I'll show you our soldiers and our statues."

"Garçon," he called out, "l'addition, s'il vous plaît."

The white-jacketed waiter came toward our table, totaling up the check with a stubby pencil which he had touched to his tongue.

Roger asked me if I was rich. I wondered if that was some rare form of old Gallic humor, but still I could think of no answer any more humorous—or appropriate—than the truth. "No . . . no, I'm not."

"All right," he said, "in that case, give me only seventy francs. I'll pay for my own espresso."

As I sneaked the money from my wallet, I kept my face averted so that he wouldn't be able to read the anger written there. Why, my father would no more let a lady pay than a man-in-the-moon! I could picture him now in the Victory Cafe sidling up to some town lady with a manufactured smile on his face while saying, "Why, honey chile, you don't think I'd let a sweet little thing like you pay for her own Dr Pepper, now do you?"

"Come on," said Roger Auberon as he began pulling me into his sprint. Ahead, a bus numbered 85 with an open-back platform waited curbside, but when we were twenty or so feet away, it started off. Figuring a bus gone is a bus gone, I tried slowing, but he would have none of that. So we continued our run until a business-suited man leaned from the back platform to catch me midsection like an intercepted football and bring me aboard. At the very next moment, Roger, with arms tautly forward like an Olympic diver, dove onto the moving platform.

"Beautiful!" I cried out, while actually applauding the display of calesthenics.

I caught him smiling as though his ego was not only being catered to, it was being satisfied. "Catching a Paris bus can be an athletic event, no?"

I answered affirmatively as the great vehicle gunned its engine and I fell back against Roger's chest. Funny thing is, I didn't too much mind being there.

The day was cool and the Paris sky like polished pewter. A good number of people, both men and women, carried umbrellas suspended from their wrists, but I knew better. There was not the slightest chance of rain. It felt instead as though God had taken on a new and challenging job as lighting technician to the world and was merely experimenting with a more theatrical method of displaying this city.

Here on the open platform, the damp wind penetrated my cardigan and although it was mildly chilling, I liked it, for it served to heighten my senses and alert me more acutely to this life. After a while, Roger put his lips next to my cheek, allowing his speaking breath to blow warm currents of air to my ear. "We are now facing the famous Avenue des Champs-Élysées."

"Oh, God, this is something," I said. "Never have I ever seen anything, anything like this. Do you know this avenue is wider than a country acre?" But as interested as I was in the dimensions of the Champs-Élysées, I was at least equally

161

as interested in the texture of his face. I wanted to touch his skin to see if it was anywhere near as soft as it seemed to be.

When the bus began making braking motions, Roger said, "We get off here." He hopped off first with the grace of a dancer and still holding onto my hand brought me along with him. Then he pointed straight ahead to an arch so magnificent that it could only designate the entrance to the kingdom of heaven.

"That," he said, "is our most famous one."

Roger must have caught my blink of blankness because he went on to explain. "About what I was telling you. How every third statue extols France's dominion over her enemies. Well, that's the most famous one of them all. The Arc de Triomphe de l'Étoile built in 1806 to commemorate the victories of Napoleon."

It was only when I went to speak that I discovered all that grandeur had left me with my mouth a-dangling. "It's so . . . beautiful."

"One hundred and sixty feet high and one hundred and fifty feet wide," said Roger with unconcealed pride. I wondered if his pride emanated from his memorization of statistics or from his quarter of a century of experience as a Frenchman beholding and ultimately coming to believe in all the power and glory remembered that is France.

As we walked along the chilled Champs-Élysées, Roger continued to hold my hand with all the delicacy usually reserved for an object of enduring value, and spoke of his country: "With all of France's imperfections, I couldn't . . . wouldn't want to live anywhere else."

Every so often, I would glance at him with his thin animated face and his lips slightly fuller and more intimate than lips have any right to be. His white dress shirt was extraordinarily soft and it looked as though it had remained frayless through countless washings only because of the skill and dedication of his washing lady. His tie was a plaid of woven wool and I just knew that it had been selected as much for its durability as for its no-nonsense good looks.

Overhead thousands of birds as undisciplined as fleeing civilians winged their way south across the dismal Paris sky. I asked Roger if they knew what they were doing since there was obviously no place better to be than this place.

He answered something which made me laugh. I would have remembered what it was except that at the moment of laughter, I caught a reflection in the polished brass of a hotel sign and I thought—thought that couldn't possibly be me strolling with the handsome photographer because the lady whose reflection I had caught was really quite beautiful.

"This is the Hotel George Cinq," he said proprietorially, as he led me inside into a world of dazzling icelike chandeliers and rugs so vibrant that they just might stand for the next one hundred years as a tribute to the weaver's art. "It's known the world over as one of the world's greatest hotels and a favorite habitat of the rich, the royal, and the military."

We found an unoccupied damask-covered sofa which Roger claimed would offer one of the finest views in Paris of "the pampered life. The columnist, Paul Robec, writing in *Le Monde,* stated that our average general spends more time in the public rooms of this hotel than they do on the battle sites of *Indochine*."

"What are they fighting about there in . . . " I hesitated only long enough to silently run through that unfamiliar word, *"Indochine?"*

Roger looked at me as though he couldn't believe that any-body full grown wouldn't know. "Oh, about the same thing that little boys and generals generally fight about: power, glory, and who gets control of the toys."

His comments scared me. They sounded so communistic . . . really unrealistic. I mean, you'd never hear my father or anybody else in Arkansas ridicule our generals. We're more patriotic than that! Of course, our farmers think there's nothing wrong with poking a little fun at Secretary of Agriculture Brannan and almost everybody, truth-to-tell, has something to say about President Truman and his daughter who thinks she's an opera singer. But then again, nobody that I know from back home would any more say a word against General MacArthur than they would against the Virgin Birth.

"Roger," I asked, already skeptical that a Jenkinsville de-fense is ever equal to a Parisian offense, "do you honest-to-goodness really believe that grown men—soldiers who know what bleeding and dying is all about—would go to war for so trivial a reason?"

"Absolutely!" answered a cheerful Roger just as though I had asked him the one thing in this world of which he was certain.

Then almost from out-of-nowhere appeared a man wear-ing the electric blue uniform of L' Hotel George V. He bent formally from the waist. "Puis-je vous aider, monsieur?"

Roger turned toward him and, with a benevolence that I wasn't sure I trusted, began speaking with a torrential river of words. I wondered if even the hotel man understood French well enough to make the word separations necessary for comprehension, but apparently he did, for he nodded his head and then with great and knowing dignity backed away.

I asked, "Well, what was all that about?"

"A hotel porter undoubtedly sent over to discreetly learn if we belong here. The management has always believed that people, like the unwashed masses that they are, would descend upon these plush premises like starving swine, unless they keep a very wary eye."

"And you don't believe that we hungry hogs would?"

Roger smiled. He was almost rakishly handsome when he smiled. "On the contrary, I'm certain that we would."

"Well, what did you tell him? Did he ask us to leave?"

"Certainly not! Ask the daughter of the American Ambassador to the republic of France and her gallant and faithful tutor, Monsieur Roger David Auberon, to leave the George Cinq? Unthinkable!"

"The WHO? The what? Now, Roger." I tried laughing. "I know that you didn't tell him that I was . . . "

"The daughter of the American Ambassador," filled in Roger while touching my knee and indicating by an elaborate roll of his eyes that somebody was approaching from the left and that now was no time, absolutely no time to talk.

From the formality of his clothes, I thought he must surely be a world-renowned concert pianist just returning from a triumphant standing-room-only performance at the Paris Opera House, but his manner spoke more of the servant *extraordinaire* than it did of the artist *extraordinaire*. He bowed low and ceremoniously to me and then spoke to Roger as an important equal.

Roger again appeared benevolent toward this new, and obviously more highly ranked representative of the hotel, while they spoke with still another swift current of seemingly non-understandable and apparently non-exhaustible words.

On taking his leave, the elegant one bowed toward me, nodded briefly at Roger, and moved toward a destination that appeared at the same time precise and unalterable.

I was afraid even to look in "my tutor's" direction for fear of showing my anger or . . . or, God help me, my amusement. A word that my parents sometimes use came to mind. *Chutzpa*. That word, I remember, was used constantly over a recent incident involving Edna Louise Jackson's mother and her long overdue bill.

Mrs. Jackson told my mother in no uncertain terms that she was "right upset" that it should even be mentioned. "After all," she concluded with an inflamed sense of self-righteousness, "my husband is the biggest landowner in Rice County and you know that sooner or later you'll be getting your money."

But the more I thought about it, the less the situation seemed similar. Mrs. J. G. Jackson is no Monsieur R. D. Auberon. He leaned toward me. "You would like a little sweet vermouth with a peel of lemon, yes?"

"Would I like a little sweet vermouth? I don't know. I guess so, but I've never drunk it. Why?"

"Oh, I thought it would be more to your taste. Personally, I prefer something a little drier, however . . . "

"However what? That's not what all that conversation was about. Ordering sweet vermouth?"

He nodded. "It was very important to the hotel management that the right drink be chosen, for they wish to offer, with their compliments, something especially pleasing to the daughter of the new American Ambassador. They referred to it as a small expression of their boundless esteem."

"But, Roger, you told them no. No thank you."

He shook his head in the negative. "No, I don't remember telling them that."

"Now this isn't one bit funny! We could get into trouble."

"With whom?"

"The police! The government! Who knows?"

"Yes? And for what violation? Drinking vermouth under false pretenses?"

"Yes, that and being an impostor!"

He laughed a deep full-voiced laugh just as though I was speaking the most incredible kind of nonsense. I wished he'd stop that laughing or that I could come inside the laughter too, but I was too nervous about the possible implications of our deception for that. What I should do is to get up and run like hell out of there! But I didn't want to . . . not without him.

Then the waiters came. There were two of them. One presented the vermouth with a flourish while the other brought forth a standing silver urn with chipped ice inside surrounding a smaller dish filled with what looked like— honest-to-God—it looked like a crystal dish filled with very small black beads.

I kept my eyes from Roger. I really didn't know what to do. Why, I hadn't even got around to knowing what to think. In America, people go to jail for all manner of things. I wondered what the French would have in mind for those who impersonate ambassadors' daughters.

Roger placed a long-stemmed glass filled with the vermouth in my hand. The next thing I recall was him refilling it. What happened to the first glass? I took another long drink. It did have a familiar fruity taste and, surprisingly, it wasn't all that bad. No, sir, it wasn't bad at all.

I closed my eyes while feeling a delightful warmth chase the last of my chill, the last of my transatlantic fear from my body. I took another long, thoughtful drink. I felt as though I had just invented health and well being. Everything was getting so lovely . . . so beautiful.

Suddenly I gave old Roger a rabbit punch to the forearm. "Two things I have to tell you. Number one. I think you're a very great and amazing fellow and number two: I think you're wonderful to look at and number three . . . what was number three?"

Then pointing out my empty glass to dear Roger David Auberon, I said, "I remember! This vermouth is number three." I heard myself breaking out into giggles. "Because it really warms up ye little cockles of me heart," I said before leaning my head back to laugh with unrestrained abandon at my absolutely extraordinary sense of humor.

· 19 ·

WHEN I OPENED my eyes, I wondered how I got here and where in God's name was here, anyway? Right off, I was aware of music, "Scheherezade," getting the full symphonic treatment. Without rising from the narrow bed, I found its source, a battered, brown radio which sat on a do-it-yourself brick and plank bookcase and also served a secondary function as a bookend to a large and carefully arranged collection of books.

This room was special. I liked the way the ceiling conformed to the pitch of the roof. The way the oversized black-and-white mounted photographs gave drama to the white-washed walls. I closed my eyes and I felt that explicit feeling of physical comfort that comes to me only when I have been freshly released from sickness.

This music, this room, this comfort. Everything was going to be okay. I stood up, letting the momentary dizziness pass before tucking in my blouse and digging deep into my purse for comb and lipstick.

Would you believe, Mother, that I'm doing this on my own? Without once having to listen to you say, "Go *verputz* yourself." But I don't want to think about you. To be honest, I had thought that by putting all this geography between us I'd have traveled far enough and fast enough to be free of both you and him. I know there's been enough distance all right, but maybe not yet enough time. That had to be it! Not yet enough time.

Before going back to my hotel, I'd have to stop at some restaurant for a really decent meal and a couple of cups of that ole sock-it-to-your-senses French coffee. Then I'd be able to figure it all out. How and why I got here.

But even now, I remember Roger and the beautiful reflection that I had made (however fleetingly) in the highly polished brass of a hotel sign. And I remembered too the Ambassador's daughter . . . that drunk-as-a-coot daughter of the American Ambassador!

From outside the room, I heard the staccato sound of footsteps climbing with quick rhythm up uncarpeted wooden steps. Then the footsteps stopped, the knob turned, the door opened, and Monsieur Roger David Auberon, wearing a smile and carrying what seemed to be France's symbol of the housewife, the heavy-duty oilcloth shopping bag, entered the room.

"You're feeling better," he said, making it not so much a question as a pronouncement.

I wondered if there was any way for any answer of mine to be non-superfluous. I couldn't think of any. "Yes, thanks. I hope I wasn't any . . . much trouble."

When he didn't immediately respond, I asked, "Well . . . was I?"

"Don't you remember anything?"

"Well," I said, actually beginning to wish for sudden and total amnesia, "I do remember getting a little high on sweet vermouth and telling jokes and—oh, God, I can't tell jokes! I never tell jokes. But I did tell them, didn't I? At least, I think I remember laughing like crazy at everything I said."

"That's true. And you remember nothing else?"

Was there something else to remember? I guess I would know if I splattered his shoes (never mind his lap!) with vomit, wouldn't I?

"You passed out," announced Roger. "After only three glasses of Cinzano. Then the hotel manager rushed over to practically insist upon informing Ambassador David Bruce at the American Embassy."

"Oh, my God, no! You didn't let him do it. I mean he didn't actually do it. Did he?"

"Well, no, he lost interest in placing the call after I admitted that you were under age and that the Ambassador abstained from alcohol."

I snapped my fingers. "How did you think of that?" I asked, snapping my fingers again.

"Mother's invention."

"Mother's invention?"

"You Americans are always saying something like that when it becomes necessary for you to do something that you have never done before."

I laughed. "Do you mean: Necessity is the mother of invention?"

"Exactly," said Roger, whose smile outshone my own. "Didn't you ever drink before?"

Didn't I ever drink before? What a question! During the eight-day crossing, didn't I have several chilled mugs of dark Dutch beer? And what about Grandmother's Passover dinners where long-stemmed wine glasses made purple by the addition of Mogen David's sweet concord grape waited for me on a hand-embroidered cloth that came all the way from Madeira. "Well, of course, I have," I told him, but when his look of skepticism didn't change, I modified, "on lots of very special occasions."

Roger now seemed more intent upon removing the contents of his shopping bag of assorted bulges than in giving a response. On a round oak table, he placed a newspaper vertically folded like a triptych, a long unwrapped loaf of crusty bread, some kind of shellfish which definitely wasn't lobster, a single lemon, a bunch of greens, a stick of butter, a conical-shaped bag fashioned from yesterday's newspaper which contained fat brown mushrooms, a pie-shaped wedge of flabby cheese, two oranges, two pears, and four eggs.

Finally looking up he said, "I think you should eat something light. Do you like omelettes?"

"Oh, yes. Very much."

Roger lifted the ugly crustacean by the bone of his back

to my eye level and for a moment, I thought he was preparing to make an introduction. "With crabmeat?"

"Uh, yes, thanks."

His pupils constricted. "You've never had crab before. Have you?"

What did he think I was, a country bumpkin? "Well, actually no."

"Never mind, the way I prepare it, you will love it! It's not for radishes that I'm the son of *le premier chef,* Edmond Auberon."

"I know," I answered, admiring in him what I lacked in myself—confidence unabashed. Then just as I was about to ask where his kitchen was, Roger bent low, pulling a low wood cart from beneath the bed. "My *cuisinière,*" he said, pointing to the shiny, meticulously arranged items within—a series of graduated pots and pans, utensils, an espresso coffee pot, and something that at first looked like a kerosene lamp without the glass chimney, which Roger identified as his alcohol-burning stove. That's a stove?

As he began preparing the food, I asked if there wasn't something I could do to help, but when he said that it's easier to do than to explain, I felt secretly relieved. He was like a culinary juggler who simultaneously sliced, sniffed, and poured while directing each action for maximum results. And, as any fool could see, this was no place for a rank beginner to join in.

The second time I asked the same question he gave a different response. "Just watch for now. In the future, there will be many opportunities to help."

That sounded like an important statement. It meant—at the very minimum didn't it have to mean—that he likes me well enough to want to spend this and future time with me? "Okay, Roger," I told him, realizing right off that my answer wasn't good enough. Not by a long shot, for it was far too fearful and too self-protective to match the occasion.

Anyway, I think I've always suffered from what I call the "Patty Bergen malady." What happens is that every time some important thing happens, my brain just ups and jams like an aged typewriter and all I can think to say is something spectacularly dumb. But this time, it didn't sound spectacularly anything. Maybe I could count that as an improvement.

Somehow I felt a little freer. "Roger, I think that was wonderful what you did. I mean, taking care of me."

Roger shrugged as with single-minded determination (not to mention patience) he picked the remaining meat from the shellfish. "It wasn't very difficult. I had the help of the hotel manager and the taxi driver. I, uh, took three hundred francs from your purse to pay the driver. Can you afford it?"

"Oh, sure."

He wiped his hands on the white dishtowel that he had tucked through his belt. "I should know better than to ask an American what she can afford." He unfolded his paper, pointed to the headline and read: "LES ÉTATS-UNIS DONNENT À LA FRANCE DE L'ARGENT POUR L'INDOCHINE. The United States gives France money for Indochina."

I wasn't sure if I had really heard the fine edge of anger in his voice. "So?"

"So, there's apparently very little that Americans cannot afford."

"I don't understand. I mean, are you saying that you don't like my country helping yours?"

Roger sighed just as though it was time to take out the garbage. "Don't you ever read the newspapers?"

"I not only read them, I work for one," I answered, hearing pride's voice. "The *Commercial Appeal*. It's Memphis's largest paper, with a paid circulation of one hundred and forty-seven thousand, and that's only on a weekday. On Sundays, the circulation is much greater."

"And your journalists, don't they speak of politics?"

"Oh, sure, they do! The last time I was in the city room, they had this bet going on. By what percentage points would Boss Crump's candidate for mayor win over his opponent, the reform candidate." And having said that, I wished that I hadn't. "Of course, not all of our political talk is only on the local level. Some of our reporters are very interested in national and even international politics."

"Then you must have heard," he said, "how France is fighting to control a small Asian country against the express wishes of the vast majority of the population."

Isn't he making too much of it? I know for a fact that America could never be a party to the tyrannization of another country. Anyway, if it was so important wouldn't it have been written up in the *Commercial Appeal*?

"Well, naturally enough," I lied, "I've certainly heard about it. It's just that I know that my country would never knowingly meddle in other people's affairs."

Without answering, Roger set the table with bamboo mats and sturdy wood-handled utensils, and lit two candles on either side of an earthen pot of mint. As he poured me a half glass of red wine, he gave me the admonition to "stay reasonably sober."

The candlelight touched only his facial ridges leaving the

rest bathed in shadows. "I wasn't planning to drink at all," I told him. "For I wouldn't want anything to blur my memory of this."

It was then that I caught the very same look of surprised vulnerability on his face that I occasionally only feel on mine. And that bit of vulnerability exposed provoked a feeling in me that was at once as unexpected as the first clap of thunder and as right as the shower that breaks a long hot, dry spell.

What I really wanted was for him to know with certainty unquestioned that there was nothing illusory about my words. The compliment, he had to know, was not only very real; it was his. All his to keep. "What I'm trying to tell you is that I'm happier being here than you know, and so I don't need or want another thing."

With studied slowness, Roger rose from his chair to look at me in a way that I couldn't (or was frightened that I could) decipher. Then for a moment, I thought he was going to move past me to change the radio's dial, but I couldn't imagine why. The music—Mendelssohn, I think it was—was really quite lovely.

Almost more with his eyes than with his hand, he reached out for my hand. And as we moved together, I came to believe that I could feel the rhythmic beat of his heart beneath the tissue-paper thinness of his cotton shirt.

"Moving with Mendelssohn," I said, wondering why I said that. And then I knew. If I could give words to this experience of closeness, then I could endow it with longevity. And one thing more. The sound of my own voice did give me a heightened sense of this is real . . . this is wonderful . . . and this is happening to me!

With his finger, he leisurely traced the outline of my lips. I don't remember ever before wanting to be kissed. But I wanted it now. As I opened my eyes to find out why it wasn't happening, I saw that he was looking at me as though "the beautiful lady" could now be found in places more permanent than the image-reflecting brass of L'Hotel George V.

As his lips moved in maddening slow motion toward mine, my eyes again closed. This time, I thought, I'm going to get something that I want. And when at last his lips reached mine, they moved me so deeply that for this moment, there was nothing else.

Then Roger's hand circled my breast and I saw in my memory a heavily perspiring revival tent minister crying out in evangelical ecstasy, "The devil saves his hottest fires for them that lusts!"

"Don't!" I cried, grabbing his wrist to break the connection.

"What's wrong?" asked Roger, looking as stricken as if he had been reprimanded.

"Nothing . . . it's not your fault."

"Tell me what happened? Why you changed? Became frightened?"

"Frightened? Yes, but not by you. Honestly, not by you!"

"Then you remembered something," he said, guiding me over to a bed covered with an Indian print fabric, "something bad from another love?"

I laughed. "Another love?" I hoped he wouldn't think I was laughing at him. "No . . . no, there has never been another love. You see, I've never . . . done anything before."

"Then what?" he asked, speaking low into my ear.

"I don't know—not exactly. Only that I was taught that this . . . that we—that what we're doing is a sin."

He brought his lips lightly to mine, then moved his head away to look at me with the most intense kind of concentration. "And what do you believe?"

I believe that those little men in their white preacher's suits spew venom along with scripture. What else have I learned from sneaking into revival tents? I have learned what it is that Protestants preach: Heaven is a very private club with an impressive sign posted across those pearly gates which reads, OFF LIMITS TO JEWS!

"Oh, God, Roger, don't ask me to think about them when I only want to think about you."

Our lips rejoined. And I felt the warming effects of a hundred glasses of *vin ordinaire* that I had never drunk.

Then our bodies began responding to a rhythm that was never scored by Mendelssohn. Something I want. Something I need. Just this once, by God, I deserve to get something I need! And it would be . . . and it would happen. And then no more alien and adrift . . . but connected and complete.

· 20 ·

THE SOFT, Paris-blue light of morning woke me, but even before the waking I knew exactly where I was and why. While drawing in the deep breaths of the still-sleeping, Roger nestled up to me as though begging warmth from my body. My arms tightened around him. Dear Roger. Sweet Roger. With you I can be free to give without having to ask what's in it for me. Only you can help me become more involved in the giving than in the getting.

I thought about that dank little revival tent evangelist now and how his under-the-arms half moons of perspiration became full moons every time he threw up his arms heavenward to plead for all those gifts that not even the Sears Roebuck catalog could provide. Go on preaching if you must. Preach on and on about the ferocity of all those fires just awaiting those that are tempted by the flesh. Preach on and on and forever and ever, but you'll never make me feel evil, not anymore. Because for at least once in my life, I am both loved and loving.

And I have just one more thing to say to you, Mister Preacher Man, one more thing: I think I may have learned something during this night that you may never understand.

As I tried with some gentleness to remove my arm from beneath the numbing effects of Roger's head, he momentarily opened his eyes. "You were happy with me, yes?" He asked before squeezing out every last bit of space between us.

"Yes," I answered, and when it struck me that I was speaking the purest kind of truth, I repeated, "Yes. Yes. And you?"

Roger grinned in a wicked way calculated to deny what his eyes were already affirming.

"You were!" I told him. "I don't care what you say, you old phony. You were happy then and you're happy now. I have ways . . . I can tell."

He blew a lock of hair from my forehead. "I was happy then and I'm happy now." Roger fixed a quick kiss on the tip of my nose before literally bounding out of bed. "But at this moment, my passion for food exceeds even my passion for you"

"Little wonder. We missed out on our crabmeat omelette."

Roger groaned. "From this time forward, I promise to contain my passion until after dinner."

Outside, the air came up with a slight cutting edge that the rising sun was already promising to blunt. If a city can be so beautiful now in September, what must she be like in April?

Roger led me over an arched bridge into an area with streets so narrow and quixotic that its planner could have given whimsy lessons to the Mad Hatter.

He pointed to a brick tricornered building with only the ground level whitewashed. "That's the place—the Café de l'Île Saint-Louis. I'll meet you there as soon as class is over. About a quarter-to-twelve. No later than noon!"

Then we kissed and as I watched him go back across the bridge, I was flooded with so much feeling for him that I had trouble remembering exactly why I had decided that this relationship had to be a temporary one.

How could I forget the obvious? Forget that there's so much that separates us. Mother, Father, please allow me to introduce my new husband. My French Catholic husband . . .

Well, why should I care what they think? Unless, is it possible even now, after everything that's happened, that I'm still trying to please my parents. Still wanting their approval . . . still needing their love.

That's not the only reason it can't be permanent. I care about Roger, but maybe he's not exactly like a man ought to be. I mean I could never in a hundred years picture my father carrying an oilcloth shopping bag or cooking an omelette or asking any woman, "Did I hurt you, my darling?"

When my father spoke, my stomach perched on convulsion's edge. Even Michael Werner was manly enough to scare me. My father and Michael, but not Roger. Not one bit Roger!

Maybe the truth is that Roger is just an imitation man.

"LIES!" My voice shrieked across the morning still. Filthy lies constructed out of revenge to punish me for my happiness.

Why is it that my father and Michael seem to me so all-fired masculine? Neither of them is particularly strong or athletic. Then what is it, this incredibly virile standard that they both represent? They look nothing alike. Everything about them is different. Their age, looks, interests, work, even the geography. No, there's absolutely nothing about the two men that's similar! Except maybe—I don't think it's that! And yet both my father and Michael seemed to experience the same kind of release after they wounded me with their easily triggered fury.

A grocer arranging a storefront bin of oranges had stopped his work to observe me. I rubbed my hand, giving out a couple of subdued cries of "oh . . . oh" just so Monsieur Grocery Man would know that when an American shouts out "LIES!" it's only because she has just been struck by some hard and painful object. Obviously!

· 21 ·

IT WASN'T UNTIL noon when I came out of the l'Alliance Française for the hundredth time—five times a week for three months is only sixty . . . not until noon when I came out of the l'Alliance Française for the sixtieth time did I realize what mischief the world had been up to in my absense.

Outside it was as though I was looking through a fine white silk screen. There was a sky full of oversized snowflakes silently gliding to earth. I took it as an omen. A first snow on the eve of Christmas eve had to be a good omen—well, if not an omen, at the very least a Christmas present.

If I walked as quickly as possible I could be back at our place in about fifteen minutes. Passing the bus stop on Boulevard Raspail, I slowed down to consider just how much faster the bus would be. On the other hand, these twice daily fares are becoming too expensive for me. I walked faster. But I also have to start conserving shoe leather. Half-soles, which are already practically an undeniable necessity, aren't cheap—at least three hundred francs everywhere I priced them. Back to the bus stop.

When I jumped off the bus in front of our four-story aged stucco building, I first peered inside Jacques's, the street-corner café, to see if Roger, who thinks of it as his own extended living room, was there, but he wasn't. Probably upstairs, I told myself, afraid that he might not be.

He wasn't there, but on the oak table was a folded sheet of lined paper with a message printed in red crayon. "Back about five. Your Roger."

Your Roger. I like that. I took off my snow dampened shoes and stockings, rubbed my cold-to-the-bone feet warm, made myself a cup of espresso, and finished off Roger's very spicy paté. It's rather nice not having him here. This way I have something to look forward to.

Also, it just might give me the time that I need. I opened my spiral notebook to re-examine yesterday's entry:

DECEMBER 22, 1950

ASSETS	LIABILITIES
1. ROGER ———————	FEAR OF MARRYING ROGER FEAR OF LOSING ROGER
2. EXACTLY 42,580 FRANCS (APPROX. $128) DIMINISHING AT THE RATE OF ABOUT 1,000 F DAILY	INABILITY TO EARN MONEY: (A) FRENCH GOVERNMENT TURNED DOWN MY REQUEST FOR WORK PERMIT (B) LACK OF JOB SKILLS
3. ENOUGH MONEY TO COVER A TRIP TO GÖTTINGEN IF I LEAVE VERY SOON	FEAR OF GÖTTINGEN
4. PREPAID STEAMSHIP TICKET LEHAVRE — N.Y.	ALONE & BROKE IN N.Y.
5. PREPAID TRAIN TICKET N.Y.C. — JENKINSVILLE	ALONE & TRAPPED & HATED IN JENKINSVILLE

SOLUTIONS ➡

HELP ME!

1.
2. ?
3.
4.
5. !

I doodled as I searched the page for solutions which had to be there, even though they always seemed ever so slightly beyond my grasp. I searched until I heard sounds on the stairs, sounds as if the building were under siege. And I knew that the only resident of 39 Place St. Sulpice who could make three flights running was now on his way up. And I guessed, even before the door opened, I guessed that he'd be smiling, and sure enough, he was.

Without a word, he set down his battered shopping bag and hung his camel-colored duffel coat on a closet hook. Then he sat down next to me. "We shall now pursue an ancient American custom."

"We're going to lynch Negroes?" I asked, remembering last night's speech which was filled with impassioned indignation after reading *Le Monde*'s account of a murder which took place outside of Hattiesburg, Mississippi.

"Tu veux être drole," said Roger more or less successfully beating back his grin. "As you can plainly see, my dear, I'm a typical American Santa Claus."

"Howdy do, Santa."

"While you," he said, bringing me to his lap, "are a typical little girl who is about to tell old Santa what you would like to have for Christmas."

"Well, old typical Santa," I said, encircling his neck with my arms: "As you must certainly realize, I've been this really terrifically sweet girl and so what I want is what I deserve. A tiara to wear to my class at the Alliance. A tiara with diamonds so large that as a source of light, it would shine in direct competition with the sun."

"Granted. The sun is now burning with envy. And now your second wish?"

186

"How many do I get?"

"Three," answered Roger with a matter-of-factness which gave a certain credence to our fantasy.

Immediately I regretted having wasted the first one with a dumb joke. "I wish for a bright red Fiat with a large wicker picnic basket filled to capacity with all the things we like to eat: cheese, paté, fresh fruit and bread, and that kind of wine you told me about."

"Lafite Rothschild."

"That's it, Lafite Rothschild! We'd eat cheese and drink Lafite Rothschild while we explored the provinces. We'd visit your folks in Normandy—why, we'd discover things we didn't even know we were looking for!"

"Excellent wish. Also granted. And now, my child, tell me your final wish."

"My final wish." Two wishes gone and I haven't begun to really get down, down to the source.

"Do I have to tell it?"

"In France, it is considered the only civilized way to make dreams come true."

It has to come true. I need it. "I've got to have a place."

"A place?"

"To belong. I have to belong to someplace . . . to someone."

Roger looked like a man who had given everything he had, only to be told that it wasn't quite enough. My dear, sweet Roger.

"You don't belong here?" he asked incredulously. "With me?"

"Yes, you know I do, or did for a little while, but time is running out."

"And I told you, we could marry."

"Marry? On what? If you were more practical, you'd understand immediately why it can't work. You can barely support yourself and your country won't even allow me to earn my keep."

"I'm not all that impractical! I have been thinking a good deal about it. I could take my photographs to every newspaper and magazine in Paris. Eventually somebody would hire me. And when we're married, the government would be compelled to issue you a work permit."

"You know, Roger, that scares me. That really scares me! Maybe I'm greedy . . . I don't know. I only know that I've grown up with only one kind of security—financial security—and you mustn't ask me to— I don't think I'm strong enough to give that up."

The silence was overwhelming. Was Roger in process of withdrawing his love? Was he thinking that I was only interested in money? In marrying any man with money? Now that's not fair!

"Roger, I feel—I know—that we should each marry someone whose life is more secure than our own. Why, even if they'd let me work, exactly what is it that I could do? This isn't my country, so please just tell me what it is that I'm qualified to do."

Finding no immediate way to dispute my words, he stared at the planks in the floor for something that seemed, if not lost, at least highly elusive. When he finally looked up again, he was almost back to the old Roger.

"Mon Dieu!" He slapped his forehead. "What kind of a Santa am I?"

"Not a particularly experienced one," I said as he raised aloft a large, cheerfully wrapped box.

"After you open it, you will see why your Christmas is coming a day early this year."

"Oh, Roger, this is really lovely of you." I pretended not to know what it was, but as recently as a week ago, he had mentioned that he was getting together an album of some of the best pictures that he had taken of me. "Then," he had said, "you will see with my eyes . . . and you will come to understand just why it is that I love you."

With as much delicacy as Scipio razing Carthage, I broke string and tore paper until the bare box lay in front of me, waiting only for a final lifting of the lid. I hesitated only momentarily, hoping that he hadn't spent any of his money on an album because any pictures that would allow me to see what it is that Roger has found to love wouldn't need any costly embellishments. When I threw off the cover, I couldn't believe what I was seeing. Is there a mistake?

"I bought you a size larger than your shoe size."

"A size larger?"

"So you should be able," he explained, "to wear them over heavy socks."

"Oh . . . yes."

"Are they all right?"

"Fine, thanks."

"If you don't like black boots, the store also has them in brown."

"No!"

"You don't like them. The style?"

"That's not true. They happen to be very attractive."

"Then what's wrong? Good God, you need them!"

"Nothing's wrong!"

"Lying doesn't become you."

I heard myself sigh as though I had just been told that I had many more miles to go and I had already gone so far. "I love the boots. It was very generous of you only . . . only I—it's so hard to explain."

"Try."

"It's the equation, Roger."

"The equation?"

"Yes, the damn equation is off balance! Can't you see?"

"Do you know what you're talking about? I don't know what you're talking about!"

"I'm talking about inequality! I'm talking about not giving enough. I'm talking about not having anything to give you."

"It doesn't matter. When you had money, you bought me things—the silk tie."

"It was nylon."

"It was silk. The label said silk."

"Roger, damnit, you spent a fortune! Who the hell asked you to go out and spend a fortune on me?"

"Nobody. It was my own dumb idea."

"Well, next time ask!"

"Why is it, Patty, when I'm good to you, you act as if a man would have to be crazy in the head to be good to you! Is that what you were taught to believe back in your home town? Jenkinsville, America? That you were unworthy of receiving good treatment? Unworthy of being loved?"

"Oh, you know that's really stupid!"

"Is it?"

"Of course. It's only that I hate to see you waste your money. And that's all!"

"Waste my money?" Roger looked incredulous. "Waste my money? Why is that? Because I chose to spend some of it on you?"

"And who do you think you are, damnit, Sigmund Freud? Well, you're not! You're nothing but a photographer. A lousy unemployed photographer!"

By the time I had walked to what looked like the Sorbonne area, my physical distress may have been even greater than my emotional distress because neither thin-soled pumps nor an unlined trench coat which had long since forgotten how to be water-repellent was ever meant for a snowstorm.

I climbed up some ice-glazed steps and from the freezing outside walked into the merely cold inside of St. Severin's. Even so I wondered if Catholicism was capable of doing as much for the spirit as this cathedral was doing for the body. I thought now about how comforting it must be to be Catholic, as years ago I had had very similar thoughts about being a Baptist. I've got to have somebody out there telling me exactly what I can and cannot do. Exactly what to believe and what not to believe.

No more maybes, buts, ifs, and if-nots. No more blurred pages or illegible scripts. If I were a Catholic, everything would be neat and clean and all spelled out.

Inside, there was a slight scattering of people. At the far side, I located an almost deserted section of pews and made a credible curtsy before entering one of them. Using my arms as a pillow, I leaned forward, letting my head rest against the pew in front. Here I can get away with it. Because here a bowed head is probably considered a sure sign of the profoundest kind of piety, while at the Café Jacques, it's considered nothing more or less than a sign of the most intense kind of intoxication.

I shivered from cold only partially relieved. It felt as though the cold had seeped clear down to the very marrow of my bones. Thawing was going to take more than a little while.

"Ah!" A sudden spasm of pain struck beneath my breastbone. It felt as though I had just been penetrated with incredible force by a poisoned-tip dart. I touched the exact point of pain while telling my—"Oh!"—while telling myself that nobody just collapses and dies of a heart attack at just turned nineteen. Ridiculous! "OHHhh . . . " Roger, Roger. I got to my feet and started a rush toward the door. "AHHhhh . . . "

While reaching out for the marble baptismal font, I felt myself crumpling. Not passing out fully, only crumpling. For there is a fire—an intense flame, the size of a pilot light, burning a hole through my heart. Please somebody, "Put out the fire . . . put out my fire!"

Hands came supporting my arms, encircling my waist. And now, finally . . . finally I could let go. . . .

· 22 ·

THE CAR DRIVEN by somebody that I didn't even try to see was going fast, maybe even recklessly fast, through the streets of Paris. In the back seat with me was a woman. Had it been her arms that had kept me from falling? "Oh . . . "

Was a stranger really taking care of me? All those times that I had been sick before, nobody had ever taken care of me. "Somebody must have said *boo* to you, Patricia." "No, Mother, nobody said *boo* to me. Honest!" "Well, somebody must have because you get sick every time somebody does."

Madame was firmly pressing my forearm. "Nous allons à l'hôpital, et quelqu'un va s'occuper de vous bientôt."

Although she was dressed in ordinary street clothes, I believe she was a nun on sabbatical. She had the clean, caring look of a nun and she was holding me as though she had no intention of letting me die. And I both believed in and took comfort from the fact that with her vast network of celestial connections, nothing could possibly happen to me without her prior consent.

Just before the car came to a complete stop, the horn began honking out the news of our arrival. Madame rubbed the back of my hand, saying that we had now arrived at the American Hospital and that I was going to receive the best possible medical care.

Car doors opened. Car doors closed. Madame cautioned the white-coated attendants who began placing me on the wheeled stretcher to *"faites attention!"* Then she ran behind the stretcher as they wheeled it up a ramp through an emergency entrance and down a corridor into a brightly lit examining room.

As my blood pressure was being taken and the beating of my heart monitored through the chilled metal disc of a stethoscope, I noted that Madame was never far away. Thank God, because no matter how many doctors and nurses were in attendance, without Madame, I would be all alone.

The doctor began asking (in real American-style English) a lot of questions such as: Exactly where is the pain? How would you describe the pain? What did you eat last?

As I pointed to the spot, I struggled to find words to convey the fearful sensation of a heart paralyzed by pain.

Then abruptly, as if he'd heard it all before, the doctor spoke to one of the attendants. "I want a G.I. series. Call X-ray. Tell them we're sending Patricia Bergen right up. Tell them that I want a flat plate of the abdomen and to give me a wet reading as quickly as possible."

"You mean . . . it's not my heart."

The doctor made reassuring taps on my shoulder. "Your heart sounds okay, but I want to keep you here in the hospital while we run some tests on your stomach."

I motioned Madame to me and this time it was I who reached out for her hand while explaining in my best Alliance-Française French about the doctor's initial findings. When I heard her sigh, I felt at the same time warmed and saddened that it was a stranger who cared that I was sick. "What's the matter, Patricia? Did somebody say *boo* to you?" Actually cared whether I would live or whether I would die.

· 23 ·

WHEN I WOKE, it was too dark to see my watch, but it felt as though it had to be not later than three o'clock in the morning. Anyway, everything began coming back in orderly procession: the argument, the freezing walk, the old church of St. Severin, my sickness, Madame, and finally this room here in the American Hospital.

I stretched out, feeling tired, but strangely exhilarated to be both warm and free of pain. I remembered too how that happened. Twice the doctor had given me a pain reliever by mouth and twice it had ended up in a pool of cream-colored vomit. But the third time, the phenobarbital bypassed the stomach for a direct entry into the bloodstream via a hypodermic needle.

Actually I couldn't believe how good I felt, especially for someone who had only hours before been given bad news. "Your X-rays, Miss Bergen, indicate the presence of a four-millimeter lesion, a good-size ulcer in the lower duodenum." Still I felt a whole lot more than merely comfortable. Sort of out there floating in phenobarbital-colored space.

And, my dear Dr. Kopelman, there's something to be said for you. Relieving me like you did (under the most honorable of conditions) of all my responsibilities.

Maybe, though, the catalyst was God himself wearing the bold black stripes of a referee and signaling down to earth: "That girl looks weary. I'm calling time out!"

Here at the American Hospital, the days passed, and I liked the way they were passing in pleasant slow motion. Outside of having to drink my cream and eat my chalk, nobody demanded anything of me. And I was neither in pain nor lonely. Roger came every evening, and during the day there was that endless bridge game in the solarium which was usually seeking a fourth hand.

The hospital library had a lot of good old stuff, and occasionally some pretty good new stuff. My favorite was a brand new book by a first novelist called *Other Voices, Other Rooms*. That one I read twice.

The door opened and Diatra, a nurse's aide from Sicily, walked through carrying my glass of cream, accompanied by two chalky pills. I made an involuntary face and Diatra responded with an if-you-only-knew-how-good-this-is-for-you face of her own. One reason, I suspect, that Diatra has such expressive looks is that she never much bothered to learn either French or English.

After she left with the drained glass, I pulled open the drawer of my bedside table to get a lemon drop which better than anything cuts the combination of chalk and cream. That's when I saw the letter. I told myself that I had already read it, and one thing is sure, this letter doesn't deserve an encore.

Before coming to the hospital last night, Roger stopped at the general delivery counter of American Express and, sure enough, they had handed him this. I slipped the letter from the envelope and despite my reluctance began reading:

January 1, 1951

Dear Patricia,

Well, I guess you sure can be real proud of yourself. You did just what you said you were going to do when you up and ran off like you did to Paris, France. Just the same, I sincerely hope that you can have a very Merry Christmas and a Happy New Year so far away from your loved ones.

I'm going to tell you the truth (your daddy doesn't think it's going to do a speck of good) as only a mother can tell it, and I sure hope you have enough understanding to take it like a daughter should.

Patricia, I beg of you to please come home for everybody's sake. We need you. I had to go to the doctor's. He put me on nerve pills, but don't worry any about me. Worry about your daddy!!! He's too proud (you know how he is) to tell you himself, but he's plenty hurt. Everybody in town knows where you are and they tease him and he tries to bear up, but it's so hard.

Like last week, George Henkins was in the store and he made a point to tell your dad that he oughta be more like him. Mr. Henkins bragged that he's the boss over his land, his niggers and his womenfolk.

Your daddy and I want you to know that we're not going to bear grudges for what you did to us. If you'll just come right on home as soon as possible, all will be forgiven. It's not too late to build a new life for yourself. Please, Patricia, because we are your parents and we do love you.

> *Love and kisses*
> *Mother*

P.S. When you write, please don't fill up your pages with any more long descriptions of churches and other buildings. You know we're not interested in that sort of thing.

I put her letter back into the drawer, took out a pen, and addressed an aerogram:

> *Mr. & Mrs. Harry Bergen*
> *c/o Bergen's Dept. Store*
> *Jenkinsville, Arkansas*
> *U.S.A.*

Dear Mother,

As you requested, this letter will be devoid of "any descriptions of churches and other buildings." What this letter will be is another serious attempt to show you why I'm unable to grant you your request to re turn to Jenkinsville.

*Just because a few people like Mr. George C. Hen-
kins razzed my father because I have traveled to a
foreign country shouldn't make either of us uncomfortable. And, anyway, since when did Mr. Henkins
(who Father himself has referred to as "a third gen-
eration high level crook") become qualified to pass
down moral judgments on others?*

*His statement to Father that he's "boss over his
land, his Negroes, and his womenfolk" says to me that
he's a more successful tyrant than Father. And I certainly wouldn't challenge the accuracy of that statement. Because it's quite true that Father is no longer
boss over me.*

*Lately, I've had a lot of time to think about things
and I have come up with at least one conclusion. And
that is that I can never again live in Jenkinsville. Now
that should, in no way, surprise you. You know that I
want to explore something more of the world and you
also know (for whatever reasons) we never did get
along.*

*At home, I remember being too often emotionally
upset and physically sick. One of the things you were
fond of telling people was that I was "the biggest
puker in town." That used to get you a few laughs.
Remember?*

*Well, what made me puke so much, I have recently
discovered, is a peptic ulcer. At this moment, I'm writing you from my bed in the American Hospital, but
by the time you receive this I will already be dis-
charged.*

*My bills are being covered by a special fund of the
American Student's and Artist's Center. I spoke with
the Episcopal minister who administers the fund and*

every time I told him that I'd pay him back as soon
as possible, he responded by telling me not to worry
so much.

I'm feeling pretty good now thanks to the really
excellent care that I'm receiving and my doctor says
that he wouldn't be surprised if my next X-ray showed
complete healing.

Now healing is one thing and preventing another
lesion from developing is quite another. Besides diet
and medication which I'll probably be on for the rest
of my life, I have to avoid high tensions and pro-
longed aggravations. So you see, there's absolutely no
possibility that I could ever again live in Jenkinsville.

I sincerely wish that I was able to help you both
with the problems that my being here has caused, but
I can't at this time help anybody else for I'm just now
learning how to help myself.

Love,
Patty

I sealed the envelope and got to remembering how I grew
up believing that I was really tough. Tough enough to
tolerate anybody's punishment. And tough enough that nobody in this world would ever be capable of destroying that
which was indestructible.

Indestructible. I know more about that now. The ulcer
taught me that there's no such thing as indestructible. It's
just another one of my Webster's International Dictionary
words. Just another word located somewhere between incle-
ment and ineligible.

The ulcer also taught me a little something about guilt.
It showed me that I didn't have to feel all that guilty anymore, for they weren't the only ones paying a price.

The door opened and Roger came into the room, lighting it up. He came directly to my bed to give me a kiss which seemed to reach deep within my body. Then he nodded back toward the door.

"I know," I told him. "You don't have to say it."

"But wouldn't you think," he said, insisting upon saying it, "that a truly civilized hospital would provide their patients with a little privacy?"

I laughed. "Only Kopelman knows for sure."

"Oh, I have something for you," he said, suddenly making me aware of the ubiquitous bag. Roosevelt had his black cape, Hitler his jodhpurs, and Roger his tote. Of all symbols, it struck me that his was the only one totally lacking in self-aggrandizement. For what is more open, more giving than a bag?

"Pears," he said, bringing out two perfectly formed ones.

"My favorite."

"I know."

"You're nice to remember that."

He looked back into the bag. A troubled look moved across his face. "There's something else."

"What?"

"I've been too busy—I never did get around to returning them." He deposited the pair of once-rejected fleece-lined black boots on my lap. "In case you haven't looked out the window, let me tell you that the real world is cold and slushy."

I felt a sudden on-rush of feeling for this man. I brought him to me, using his shoulder to rest against. "You're easy to love."

"I want to be . . . for you."

"I mean, I've only known you for a few months."

"Almost four."

"And I've known them all my life and yet you give me so much more. You're a much finer person than they are! I know that now. Why, do you think my father would care if my feet were dry? I can't imagine that he would. So, if you're the better man, then why do I consistently use him for the standard? He's a lousy standard!"

Roger shrugged. "He's all you've known. We French have a saying, 'Nous marions nos propres couchemars.' "

"We marry our own nightmares?"

"That you are destined to seek from a husband what you have already experienced from a father."

I thought about that until I thought I heard a slight knocking sound. There it was again, shy and tentative. "Oui," I called out, "entrez."

The door opened a wedge and then a face, a woman's face that I had seen before but couldn't immediately identify, emerged. "Est-ce que je peux entrer?"

I did know her! That's the same face. It was Madame, who kept me from collapsing at the church's baptismal font and comforted me all the way to the hospital. Surprisingly, she was a good deal younger than I had remembered (or to be still more accurate, probably needed to believe). "Oh, my God, yes it's really you! Of course, you may come in," I said, waving her enthusiastically toward me.

Now her step quickened, losing all hesitancy. She was now approaching me as though we were very old friends, who had only inadvertently been separated by time or space. We embraced and then we laughed and embraced once again.

"Vous allez bien?" she asked. "N'est-ce pas?"

"Oh, absolument. Merci beaucoup pour votre assistance—oh," I said, turning to look at Roger, who seemed a lot less surprised than I felt. "This is who I told you about. The lady that I thought I'd never get to thank because I never learned her name."

Roger stood and, with a kind of easy dignity, introduced himself and then for the first time, I heard her say her name . . . Olivia Marcou. It was Olivia Marcou.

She explained that she had been wanting to visit me for some time, to see how I was getting along, but her employer at the stationery store had been keeping her late.

I heard myself expressing genuine surprise that she worked. Oh, I knew even as I said it that it sounded dumb, but I never thought of her as actually working. Unless, of course, she was Mother Superior of an orphanage or something extraordinarily useful like that.

That's when it struck me that surprisingly, since she was so important to me, I knew practically nothing about Olivia Marcou. I didn't know if she was married or single. Did she have children? How many and how old? Did she love them? A lot?

And I wondered about Olivia Marcou as a little girl—the games she played and the toys she cherished.

No, I didn't know the first thing about her. Or maybe I did know the first thing. And the first thing became everything: When I needed her, she was there.

· 24 ·

BEFORE BREAKFAST on Friday, Dr. Kopelman strode into my room carrying an X-ray and two booklets which he deposited on my lap. *Eat Well to Stay Well* cautioned one, while another one, titled *Taking Care of Your Ulcer,* pictured a radiantly smiling man on the cover.

"Well, well, well," he said, blowing cigar ashes off his red-and-green checked tie, as he seated himself in the cushioned chair next to my bed. "Tomorrow, you graduate."

"Tomorrow?" I asked, already feeling the chilling winds of the January world. It wasn't as though I was surprised. It was only that I hadn't been expecting it. Well, exactly what did I expect? This is, after all, a hospital and not a home for little wanderers.

Ted Kopelman looked downright pleasant. "Yep, but I'm going to give the commencement address right now." He went on to tell me what a grave mistake it would be to ever underestimate an ulcer's potential for destruction. Particularly when it developed in one so young. How my life has to be so disciplined that I can never again put food in my mouth without first determining whether it's on the approved iist.

And when the doctor spoke of cigarettes and booze, he reminded me of the Reverend Mr. Burton Benn's zeal while addressing himself to the subject of lust and greed.

After we wished each other "goodbye and good luck," Dr. Kopelman left and I felt my empty gut begin to suffer abrasions from rubbing against the breastbone. I threw a couple of chalky pills into my mouth and tried, with my most reassuring voice, to calm myself down.

It's all right to be a little upset. It's never easy being forced from a safe harbor. A safe harbor, nothing! This place is more like an institutional mother to me.

That's when I began to laugh out loud. God, if anybody here ever found out that I have a filial attachment to the American Hospital, then they'd ship me upstairs to the psychiatric ward for sure.

Boy, I'm really something! I mean if on my birthday I gave myself a tape recorder with a few prerecorded messages such as: "Everything's gonna be all right" and maybe another message saying "Lay down your sweet head, honey babe, and rest a spell," then by Mother's Day, I'd be, sure enough, sending that machine a dozen long-stemmed American beauties.

By the time Roger arrived, I knew exactly what it was I had to do. I just didn't know how. How to break it to him. But we didn't get around to talking about it. At least not right away because he came in all consumed by his opportunity to buy a bargain motor scooter—a Vespa with barely three thousand miles on it.

"Not a lot of power," he was saying, "but very reliable. It could take us to Normandy, the south of France, and across to the Italian Riviera."

"I'd love it! The sun, the wind, even rain! I wouldn't even mind a little rain—honest! And fog! Fog so deep and mysterious you could get lost in it. But sometimes you'd have to let me drive too. You would, wouldn't you?"

"Any time," said Roger, smiling so broadly that I didn't know whether or not he was sincere. He spoke of a two-man tent he'd seen. (I didn't bother correcting the error of his gender.) "Very lightweight and compact. Every night," he concluded, "we will lie together under the birds."

"Stars," I quickly corrected.

"Stars," agreed Roger, before breaking away from his vision. "Has Dr. Kopelman said anything specific about being released?"

My stomach lining felt as though it had just been attacked by a particularly ferocious square of very coarse-grained sandpaper. "He came by this morning—I'm not positive about the time." That statement was hastily calculated to bore, or better still to mislead. At least until I can figure out how on this earth I'll be able to tell him what it is that I know I have to tell him.

Roger, though, was not put off. He was directing all of his energies toward knowing. "Tell me what he said."

I resisted the temptation to look away. "Said?"

"About your leaving here!"

"He—Dr. Kopelman—said that he was releasing me in the morning."

"Magnifique!" he cried, wrapping his wiry arms around me like so much ribbon around a Christmas gift. "To be together again!" Then he suddenly pushed me an arm's length away as though the wrappings had a need to examine the gift. "What else? What else did he tell you?"

"Nothing that I didn't already know. That I would have to live a carefully regimented life."

He was looking me over very carefully. "I don't believe you. He did tell you something else!"

"No. At least not what I think you're implying. The ulcer has healed without complications. The great Kopelman himself referred to it as an unremarkable recovery. It's only . . . "

"Only what?"

"Only that I have to make you understand something, but I have no way—no words to make you understand."

A vertical line as definitive as an exclamation mark sliced his forehead into almost equal sections. "Understand what?"

"What it is I have to do."

"Which is?"

"I have to go to Göttingen—in Germany."

"Göttingen," Roger blinked. "In Germany."

Progress was being made. "Yes! Yes!" I cried out, encouraged. "That's where I have to go tomorrow as soon as I'm released. If I wait, I won't have enough money for the trip. Now you may think that this is a rash and foolish thing to do, but all I can tell you is that it isn't rash. I've thought about it for six years!"

Roger's forehead crease deepened. "Why are you all of a sudden discussing Germany? You never before mentioned Germany. Are you feeling dizzy? Did the doctor give you an injection?"

"No, I'm not dizzy and no, there's been no injection! I'll start from the beginning. That way it will be easier for you to understand."

But how can I make him understand? How can I possibly explain to Roger what I've never been able to explain to myself adequately? "It was the year that I was twelve. A German prisoner-of-war camp was set up near our town of Jenkinsville and then . . . well, what happened was . . . " I could still feel some of the same feelings that I felt then, only now I have lost all the words. Where did I put those words?

"Ah, yes," said Roger, looking at me in a way that I didn't understand because I had never seen that particular look on his face before. "And now you wish to visit some German soldier? Someone who was very special to you, n'est-ce pas?"

Could it be that he's jealous? He was sounding jealous.

"Roger, I was only twelve years old!"

He bumped his fist against his lips. "Sorry. Continue, please."

"Well, one really hot day, some of the prisoners began passing out in the cotton fields. You don't know how hot it can get in Arkansas! Once I remember it was so hot that I

209

turned on our garden hose and the water that came out gave me a first-degree burn. And another time—"

"Patty, tell me about Germany."

"Ah, yes, well . . . As I said, the prisoners began passing out in the cotton fields. So the guards took a bunch of them into town, into our store, for field hats. And that was how I happened to meet him. How I happened to meet Frederick Anton Reiker. From the first moment that I saw him, I knew . . . knew that he wasn't like them. Like the others."

"Chose qui plaît est à demi vendu!"

"It wasn't just his looks! Oh, I loved his looks, but more important, he was a wonderful man. And a pacifist, like you."

"He convinced you of that? Every son-of-bitch Nazi soldier who got trapped in Paris after the occupation swore on God's good name that he wasn't like the others!"

"Roger, don't you know that you never have to give a Jew lessons in German-hating?"

Roger made a few more bumping motions against his lips and I continued. "And anyway, jealousy is wasted on the dead." I took his hand to kiss the inside of his palm. "It's okay, I know you suffered a lot during the occupation. But Anton also suffered. I have always considered him as much a victim of the Nazis as Grandma's family from Luxembourg. Well, after Anton escaped, I saw him just about dusk running along the railroad embankment and that's when I took after him and hid him in some old abandoned rooms above our garage."

"That was just after the war?"

"No, during. During the war."

"Didn't you realize that you could get into trouble with the authorities if you were caught?"

"Of course! Of course, I realized. I'm not dumb, you know! In my life, I've been confused, and I've vacillated a lot, but I've never NEVER been dumb!"

Roger's shrug seemed to involve his whole body. "You know that isn't what was implied."

"I hope not, because I feel strongly about it. You see, some people—my lawyer, for instance, tried to build an entire defense on the proposition that I was dumb and simply couldn't comprehend the consequences of my actions."

"Your lawyer? You did get into trouble with the authorities?"

"Well, yes . . . some. It wasn't all that bad. I guess what I minded as much as anything else was the people on my side, like my grandparents, who were patronizing on the same basis as my lawyer. My father, now that I think of it, at least understood that I knew what I was doing. But for everybody else being twelve made me some kind of a dummy. Well, I wasn't dumb and I did know!

"And even now I still feel a sense of pride, knowing that I did the best I could for him. Even after he died that helped. Oh, I cried about a beautiful person losing his life and I cried for myself . . . for all I had lost."

He gave short nods of his head. "Without an understanding of the inherent risks, your sacrifice would be without value."

"Exactly!" I said, squeezing his hand. "Without an inherent value I—I . . . say that again, please."

"Certainly. If you did not understand the inherent risks

that you took on behalf of this man, then your sacrifices would be diminished."

"Oh, my God, Roger, you know so much!" I cried out, grabbing his hand. But it wasn't until I saw him wince that I realized my nails were cutting hard into his palms.

"Well, I don't understand everything. If Frederick Anton Reiker is dead, then why go to Göttingen?"

"That's the most difficult part of all to explain."

As he rested his chin against an open hand, I could tell that he was preparing himself for a period of intense concentration.

"I can tell you that it has something to do with what I don't have. With what I've never had . . . with . . . "

"Is it so difficult," asked Roger with the most annoying kind of serenity, "to confide in me?"

"Damn right! And it's hard for you too, and don't you forget it! Exposing oneself isn't easy, not for anybody. Maybe it's particularly difficult for me. I don't know. But all my life, it's been so very important to avoid showing any weakness. I felt as though I had to appear invincible just to survive. And breaking old habits is still difficult."

"But you know you can trust me," said Roger. "Whatever it is, I'll understand."

"Don't think it's bad! It's really nothing that's bad. It's not as though I've killed or stolen. Why, I never even break in line, drop gum wrappers on the sidewalk, or renege on library fines."

Roger nodded with what appeared to be a solemnity concocted to match the occasion.

"Then why—please tell me why I'm so ashamed of it, Roger?"

"I don't even know what you're talking about."

I heard myself sigh just as though I were experiencing a rapid and complete energy depletion. "For a while, all the time I was with you, I thought that I had given my old obsession the slip."

I caught Roger smiling as though I were a frightened child needing only a few moments of his parental reassurance. "You've never experienced an obsession! Well, let me tell you, my friend, if you're ever given the choice between an ulcer and an obsession, grab the ulcer. That only affects your body. While an obsession takes over your whole life."

He wrinkled his forehead. "An obsession is affecting your life?"

"Not just affecting, Roger! Controlling. Controlling my life! Compelling me to do what is, at the same time, frightening and embarrassing."

He shook his head. "I can't believe—"

"You can believe because I'm telling you! This is not the sort of thing that anybody would get pleasure from making up. But before I tell you what it is—what the obsession is—I want you to know that the only time I really had it under control was the time I spent with you. At least that's what I believed until Olivia Marcou. But understand, she didn't create my monster, she merely revived it. So, I think that I'll never be fully comfortable until I . . . "

"Yes?"

"Until I follow it—the experience—to its conclusion. Whatever that conclusion may be. Now, do you understand?"

"I'm not sure I understand anything."

"Oh, my God, Roger, weren't you listening? How could anyone be any clearer than that? What I'm trying to tell you is very simple. When Olivia Marcou comforted me on the way to the hospital, I knew that I had to be a part of a . . . had to have a family!"

"Aha!" said Roger, tapping his own chest. "Allow me, madame, to show you exactly where a most exceptional husband can be found who with pleasure and pride will join with you in the creation of beautiful little children. Et violà! Ta famille."

"Oh, no, Roger, no! Is that what you think I'm talking about—marriage?" I heard the word *marriage* spill from my tongue with a sharp, twisted kind of shrillness. "I'm not ready for that! I don't know how to be what I've never had! I don't want to *be* a mother. I want to *have* one. Don't you understand I want Anton's mother to be my mother too!"

I watched Roger carefully ease himself into the bedside chair as though he too had been recuperating from a very long and debilitating illness. Then he adjusted his polished metal watch strap. Releasing the catch and closing it. Releasing and closing. Closing and releasing. I felt the tension pull all of my own nerves into a thin, taut line. Releasing and closing . . .

Then his hand moved away from the watchband to press for a few moments against the inner corners of his eyes. He looked directly at me. "Tomorrow morning," he said in a voice heavy with leaden authority, "I will come to the hospital to take you home. You will recover your strength and in the spring we will tour France and some of Italy from our Vespa."

I had just enough courage to use his name, but not enough to look at him. It wasn't his face anyway. I know because Roger's face held such an enormous capacity for joy and what I was now hearing was infinities removed from joy. "The problem is, Roger," I explained, "that if I leave for Göttingen tomorrow then I think I'll have just enough money to cover the trip to Göttingen and then back to the States. But the catch is that I simply can't afford to spend another franc in Paris."

"I deserve better treatment than this!"

I heard the words all right, but they didn't sound like his words, for they were too harsh and alien sounding to have emerged from his lips. "What?"

"Why do you stare at me as though you don't understand? Do you wish me to repeat? *Certainment.* If that's the way you felt, then why hold on to me? Unless you are an opportunist, why wait until the last possible moment to tell me of your plans?"

"Because I only found out myself this morning after Dr. Kopelman told me that I was being released."

"You think I'm going to believe that? For twenty-two days you have nothing to do but rest and think and then today, at the very last moment, you make this incredible decision! Is that what you're telling me?"

"Yes! Yes, that's what I'm telling you. Why do you doubt me? What ulterior purpose could I have?"

"To hold on to me, dear lady, until I no longer had function for you. Lady, I admire you. You are shrewd!"

"Look, Roger, I know you're disappointed, but I don't think you know . . . or even believe what you're saying."

"Oh, I know . . . I know! But you don't know what you're doing! You're leaving me. We love each other—I thought we loved each other, but you're leaving. And for what? Answer me! For WHAT?"

"I tried to explain it. You told me to trust you, Roger. Told me that you'd understand."

"Oh, I understand!" he shouted. "I understand!" But his face was so consumed by rage that I doubted that there was enough leftover space there to squeeze in a little understanding. "And I hate what I understand."

"Oh, please don't, Roger! And don't hate me—I can't stand the idea that we'll part in anger."

"Better try to get used to it because I feel more hate for you than I can tell you. You are cold . . . money hungry . . . and very, very calculating."

"That's not true!"

"It's true," he said in a voice that could be used for the most ordinary of business transactions. "Love isn't nearly good enough for you. You want money too. A husband with very much money!"

"I never said that!"

"And there's something else I could tell you," said Roger, shifting back into a more comfortable stance. "I suspect that your poppa may be doing exactly the right thing as he chants those Hebrew prayers of the dead over you."

· 25 ·

CONSIDERING ALL THE trouble I had falling asleep, I didn't expect to wake again either so soon or so abruptly, but an ongoing wave of nausea along with the distinct smell of blood rising from my breath encouraged me to snap on the light and move as rapidly as possible through the hospital room toward my connecting closet-sized bathroom. I reached it just in time to see a glob of blood falling from my mouth like a crimson waterfall.

At the first respite, I held tightly to a metal support bar and felt my temperature soar to heights that no thermometer could follow. I reread with sudden interest the sign posted conspicuously above the washbasin:

PRESS BUZZER
FOR ASSISTANCE

Roger. Somebody. Somebody please, please help me. I watched the large sign blur and then darken. The buzzer was within reach, but I couldn't risk releasing even one hand from the support bar.

Another rush of nausea, and I tenuously held on while opening my mouth wide to make way for the painful passage of still another bloody geyser.

Then it came to me what was happening! The ulcer had perforated and I was hemorrhaging.

PRESS BUZZER
FOR ASSISTANCE

And there was a chance, I wondered if it was a likely chance, that I'd never see another day. It didn't seem like such a big deal, and yet I was feeling sorry for myself. Nineteen is too young to die. I didn't want to leave such an unfinished life. With more time, I might have been able to make a better job of it.

Mostly I wanted to leave somebody behind on this earth who would mourn me. Without that it would be as though all my years and all my pain had counted for nothing. As though I had never lived at all.

Would Roger find out? Who would there be to tell him? And if he did find out, would he mourn? Oh, how I'd want him to! Partly out of revenge. He would suffer as he has made me suffer.

My parents? I think they'd care, but I don't think they'd care very much. Anyway how many times can you sit *shiva* for the same person?

My grandparents would care and Sharon might care a lot. And Ruth, oh God, how Ruth would care! I hurt at the sheer quantity of pain that I have already caused her. But I hope it's like she says, that I've given her something too. Only I wish I could remember what it was.

More immediately I regretted the globs of blood that landed on the toilet seat and the even larger puddle at my feet. "Who was it that said *boo* to you, Patricia?" "Nobody said *boo* to me, Mother, honest!" Would the hospital staff consider that indicative of an uncaring (although now deceased) slob? And so good riddance to her! Please don't. Don't think that about me because, truth is, I haven't strength anymore even for holding on.

Also I regretted the way my cotton nightgown was now plastered to me by heavy sweat. It seemed like a particularly unlovely, not to mention unfeminine, way in which to be found dead.

A sudden chill which raised all my goosepimples was now superimposing itself upon the sweat.

PRESS BUZZER
FOR ASSISTANCE

I am reaching beyond my capacity to endure pain. Somebody's got to help me. I am afraid of dying. I am afraid of dying alone. Please come to me, Roger. Tell me that I will live. Tell me that everything will be all right. And don't forget to tell me too that your words were only lies . . . only jealous lover lies.

The walls whirled by in a blur as though I were observing them from the side window of a speeding Paris taxi. I saw the moving sign—the bold black letters smearing across the white background as it went rushing by. Even so I knew what it said:

PRESS BUZZER
ROGER'S
FOR ASSISTANCE

I saw my hand reach out to touch the buzzer, but nothing sounded. Sign swiftly speeding. Again my hand reached out to find the buzzer and then I heard it. Heard a very audible buzz.

Dr. Kopelman pulled back my eyelid and peered with a lighted instrument into my eye. "Don't mind me, sweetheart; I'm just admiring your beautiful eye."

"Ohh." I had tried to smile, more for Dr. Kopelman's benefit than from any overwhelming need of my own for comic relief, but I immediately regretted the effort, for I discovered that even a smile had the power to intensify the pain.

"How do you feel?"

"Sick."

He patted my hand. "We gave you a shot and that will help ease the pain. And we're setting up a blood transfusion. That will help too."

As I slipped a sky blue sweater over my head two weeks later, Dr. Kopelman came into my room to give his "commencement address, part II." Then the internist abruptly stopped his lecturing to make the observation that I looked "very pretty. Really nifty in street clothes."

Dr. Kopelman brushed some invisible lint from his tweed jacket before saying that he didn't want to frighten me, but that he would be "unforgivably remiss" if he failed to warn me that "a hemorrhaging ulcer constituted a life-threatening situation" and that I had to do everything possible to prevent a recurrence.

"I'll cater to my ulcer exactly as you taught me, Dr. Kopelman."

He handed me some neatly stapled mimeographed sheets of paper. "Your diet and your instructions. Notice that rule number one concerns the duration of bedrest. For the first two weeks at home, I want you to stay pretty close to your bed. Total relaxation is what you must have. Physical and mental relaxation!"

I located a taxi at the hospital's front door, but every time the meter clicked, I tried telling myself with monumental calm that money is only money. And I'm not worried. Anyway, taking the bus on this January day in my condition would be nothing less than an offbeat form of suicide. As it is, Kopelman would probably break our patient-doctor relationship if he knew that within less than two hours, I had every expectation of being on that train to Göttingen. I wondered if my doctor would be mollified a little bit if I bought a first class ticket.

At 39 Place St. Sulpice, I confided to the driver that I was "très fatiguée" and that, if he didn't too much mind maybe he oughta see to it that I got up the three flights. I also ex-plained that it would take me only a few minutes to pack and from here we'd go directly to the railroad station.

I knocked at the door to our place so tentatively that even the driver commented that only a trained bird dog could have heard it. Then he gave the door a single vigorous whack. When there was no response, I inserted my key into the lock, feeling inordinately relieved that I wouldn't have to face Roger and profoundly saddened that I wouldn't get to see him.

· 26 ·

THE LOBBY of the Hotel Göttingen with its castle-style oak furniture, tapestries of hunting scenes, and leaded glass windows looked every bit as respectable (and infinitely more old world) than the sanctuary of the Jenkinsville First Baptist Church. Good. I was going to need every millimeter of respectability I could get.

The porter, a man too wizened and old to be carrying his own let alone other people's bags, showed me into a large

223

room with a massive bed embellished with elaborate carvings. In the bathroom, he curiously turned on both faucets and smiled idiotically when water gushed through the pipes. Actually, I don't think he began smiling idiotically until I placed a bunch of strange-looking coins in his hand.

That's when I realized that in my nervousness to give enough, I must have outrageously overtipped him. So be it! I'm not going to worry about it now. Still I can't afford to go around doing that again. Repeat after me: Spending marks is just like spending real money. And again: Spending marks is just like spending real money.

He quietly closed the door behind himself and I was alone, just me and the telephone. With any luck that slim gray volume beneath it would be the city of Göttingen telephone directory. And so it was. As I lifted the booklet, it opened more or less automatically to the Rs. Rabe, Radis, Radloff.

A lot of the Rs were listed as professors. I guess that's to be expected in a town that houses one of the oldest universities in the world. Reicher, Reichert, Reider. How old did Anton say this university was? Reiker! Reiker, Prof. E. C. Buhlstrasse 64 . . . 7688

I sat down on the bed, cradled the phone in my arms, and warned myself that this was no time to panic. Just take it easy now. Get the feel of the phone. See, not that different from American phones. No rush. After six years of waiting, what's another few minutes?

Then the room grew uncommonly warm so I took off my coat and unzipped my new fleece-lined boots. My watch, which runs maybe five minutes fast, said 4:18. So, it's only 4:13 P.M. I tried picturing exactly what she might be doing now, now at this very moment. Preparing dinner for her family? Maybe also for a few of her husband's distinguished colleagues who are visiting from a very distant and celebrated university.

It's dinner-cooking time. The worst possible time to call! The turkey needs basting, the soup needs stirring, and the table needs—LIES! I'm sitting here scaring myself to death with lies. It's not that way at all. Colleagues don't come in all that often, and Wednesday isn't a popular night for a feast.

No, Mrs. Reiker is sitting alone in a favorite wing chair; the lowering afternoon sun speckles the carpet and the arm of her chair. Directly in front of where she sits is an ottoman slipcovered in matching blue linen, but she has no use for an ottoman. Her feet are planted firmly on the floor. But what is far more interesting than where her feet rest is her gaze, which seems completely unlimited by mere architectural considerations. Roof, walls, none of it matters when what you're seeing isn't what is, but what was. What once was . . .

How he must have filled that room! Anton six years dead. Six years is plenty long enough to soothe the tearing anguish of his death, but maybe no amount of time is enough to soothe something that is no longer there. Something like an emptiness that can never be filled because it's only a bit of space carved out of air.

That's it! What I didn't understand well enough to explain to Roger! I think maybe I could make him understand now. I'd simply tell him: Mrs. Reiker and I, we're so much alike, suffering as we do from this . . . this nothing. So you see, Roger, I feel—I know that by Mrs. Reiker's and my pooling our remembrances, we'd both learn to constrict the immovable void.

Suddenly I felt depleted by a combination of hospital lethargy and unaccustomed exertion. I placed the phone back on the bedside table, flipped off my boots, and flopped back across the bed.

When I woke in a darkened room, my stomach let me know that it had been neglected and that a little food was now in order. Kopelman's third rule: Eat small, but frequent, meals. Always keep something in the stomach.

It was a little after eight o'clock when I left the dining room of the Hotel Göttingen with the sense of well being that comes from eating a fine dinner and drinking a little wine. Dr. Kopelman may be perfectly right about alcohol, but he's wrong about a little wine. Why, without that wine, I don't know if I could calm down enough to place the call.

The elevator operator, a strong, solemn man who apparently spends an inordinate amount of his income on hair grease, jumped to his feet in military fashion to guide me inside the well-polished wood-and-brass cubicle. I wondered how many other Jews he had guided . . . only to less pleasant destinations. Animal!

"Finif," I called out, wondering if he would recognize my specific dialect of German as Yiddish. If only I could also say in the dialect of my ancestors, "Please sir, I beg of you—don't harm my children!" Maybe he would have remembered hearing that during his soldiering days.

I unlocked the door to room 515, snapped on the bedside lamp, and consulted the telephone directory. Seven-six-eight-eight just like before. I took the phone into my lap, and let

226

my index finger get in a little practice by falling into the appropriate holes without actually dialing them. I noticed an unmistakable tremor in both hands, but seemingly more pronounced in my right hand. I'm confident that will not present any real problem. I'm not the least bit worried about that!

My finger can still dial, but what then? Don't panic, just stay as calm as I am now because nothing's really difficult. All very simple. Keep telling myself: all very simple, very natural. When the phone is answered simply say, Mrs. Reiker, please. Shouldn't I say, *Frau* Reiker? No! Then she'll begin answering in German and then where will I be?

Not so. When she hears my accent, she'll immediately revert back to her Manchester, England, English. Maybe, but what if she doesn't? Doesn't realize that I can't speak the language? What if she considers my lack of response simple rudeness? A university student playing a practical joke? With a controlled, but very real, aristocratic anger, she'll hang up. And, at that moment, our connection will be broken for all time.

My stomach began burning mildly and I wondered if it was from the wine or from the stress: I dialed room service and after what seemed an endless wait, a woman's voice answered, saying something. Not a word of which I understood.

"Milchik," I said, at the first pause.

She answered with a question of her own which I partly understood, partly only guessed at. I supplied my name and my room number and when I heard her say, *"Bitte,"* I knew that she had understood.

As I hung up, my stomach began to swirl like a just-flushed toilet. I reached the bowl just in time to unleash a river of wine (but no blood—thank God, no blood!). I staggered back to the bed while giving an endorsement to the absent. "I should have listened to you, my dear Dr. Kopelman. You told me, in no uncertain terms, to especially avoid the double As: alcohol and aggravation." Oh, God, why the hell can't I learn to listen?

It's not that I don't listen. It's that (in spite of all the evidence) I have a hard time believing that I am actually vulnerable.

I've felt invulnerable—completely invincible for such a long time. At least as far back as Miss Judith Hope Dixon's third grade. I remember it was Miss Dixon's overgenerous arithmetic assignment that I was working on one evening at our dining-room table. The room was lit by a small crystal chandelier which had three candlelike bulbs, each giving out a candleful of light.

To make dimness even dimmer, every time I would lean over my book, I'd block out what little light there was. Suddenly I yelled up at the chandelier, "The dumbest thing anybody ever did was to go and buy you!"

Then it happened: My father rushed through the door. I looked up just in time to see his extended palm fly toward my cheek. I screamed as the slap threw me off the chair and against the wall.

"How dare you question what I spend my hard-earned money on," he cried out. "You goddamn ingrate!"

He stood there with his feet apart, staring down at me as though he were the just-proclaimed heavyweight champion of the world, and I were the evil scum he had defeated. Even so, I understood that his full release from tension could not come until I totally dissolved into sobs so hysterical and un-controlled that there would not be the slightest question of my defeat.

And so only by concealing my own pain could I deny him what he needed. If I refuse to concede defeat, then how can he celebrate victory? I sucked in my tears to look at him directly and full-faced, because it was very important for us both to understand that nobody, not him or anybody else, could ever destroy that which is indestructible. Me.

At the door there was a knock, low and discreet. I rose while cautioning myself, "Spending marks is just like spending real money," and opened the door on a gray-haired woman wearing an almost identically colored uniform. With well-practiced efficiency, she set down a tray containing a white porcelain pitcher of milk emblazoned with a bit of heraldry, a crystal glass, a white cloth dinner napkin, and two sugar cookies.

I sipped the milk and felt it coating my burning gut with cooling substance. By the time I began congratulating my-self on a really remarkable recovery, it was 9:40 P.M. and too late to call.

In Jenkinsville, anyone who hears the phone ringing past nine or nine thirty automatically becomes a little fright-ened. Tomorrow, first thing in the morning, will be soon enough. If I hadn't won an actual victory, I had at the very least won the next best thing—a temporary reprieve.

Inside my window, the square panes were becoming opaque from frost. I pressed my palm against the glass and watched a thin ribbon of icy water race down. I kept wiping away errant ice and excess water until I had what I wanted:

a sort of oblong bit of clarity which allowed a sugar-glazed, white magic view of the city.

Göttingen was quiet and softly lit; a few cars drove slowly down narrow snow-edged streets, passing a few heavily garbed and briskly walking people. In the square across the street was a larger-than-life statue of a young girl standing steadfastly under an ice-coated canopy of wrought-iron wildflowers. And in each frozen hand she was clutching a perfectly enormous goose.

It wasn't until I looked up, though, that I really saw this city. Rows of frosted tile roofs topped narrow stucco and half-timbered buildings, and just ahead was a tower so obviously medieval that its stones had to have come from quarries now long forgotten. Everything seemed very familiar and yet I had never seen anything like this before except . . . except maybe in a certain picture book which was showing advanced signs of age long before it was passed on to me.

And years after I grew too old for picture books, I still loved that book, *Tales from Far Away Places.* It told how a poor cobbler's apprentice slew the dragon and saved the kingdom, and how the king lost and then regained his virtue. It also told of a lonely girl who ran away from her cruel stepmother, only to wander over many miles and face many hardships before finally finding her real mother. The one who loved her.

· 27 ·

AFTER A COMFORTING dream-filled night, I woke just before the breaking of dawn. For a while I lay in bed unsuccessfully trying to recapture even one of those nighttime visions. But just because I can't recall it doesn't mean that I didn't experience it, and I'm going to cling to my good dream aura like a good omen.

It didn't take me long to bathe and dress because even before leaving the states, my decision on what to wear on this day had already been made. I'd given it a lot of thought. It had to be respectable without being boring and it had to convey the impression that I'm not there to take anything that isn't mine. Because obviously I don't have to.

Before punching the elevator's down button, I allowed myself a long, thoughtful look in the almost full-length hall mirror. The vibrant pink blouse that I wore under the charcoal gray jacket and pencil thin skirt was good looking, and more important, I looked good in it. Even my figure, I'll have to admit, wasn't half-bad.

Now where was that elevator? Maybe I should save time and take the stairs; it's only four flights down to the hotel's street-floor restaurant. Dumb idea! In my present recuperative state, that would consume roughly my entire day's ration of energy.

When the elevator door opened before me, I checked my watch. Not yet eight o'clock and phone time is still more than two hours away.

But two hours or two minutes or two years, it was all future time and I wanted to concentrate on this time. Maybe this moment is my moment of triumph because, for better or worse, I have done exactly what it was that I set out to do one-third of my life ago.

At the double doors of the dining room, I was greeted by a gentleman wearing a black bow tie. He would have struck me as being extremely dignified except for one thing—he bore a certain resemblance to Harpo (or was it Chico?) Marx.

I hadn't realized it last night, but the dining room of this venerable hotel offered a fascinating street-level, leaded-glass view of the city. I was seeing what Anton had once

232

seen. And that's when it happened. I felt touched by fresh grief from a very old wound.

It was like that. Sometimes I'd go for a period—days or weeks—without feeling the full sweep of my loss, and then as unexpected as a thunderclap, the realization would rip the protective coating from my senses. Maybe that's the way it is with trick knees and aging griefs. Totally pain free one moment and absorbingly painful the next.

The white-jacketed waiter brought me my eggs (over light), a pewter pot of very hot coffee, and a mahogany bread tray filled with thick slices of rye and almost black pumpernickel. The bread was honest bread, all right, but ah . . . the coffee was wonderful. So much better than French coffee, which is so strong that only masochists and philosophers even claim to like it.

By nine thirty, all the coffee had been drunk, the eggs and most of the pumpernickel eaten. Time to go back upstairs and prepare for the call.

In my hour-and-forty-minute absence, the maid had already cleaned room *finif-eins-finif*. Another good omen? I smiled (laughter almost never happens to me when I'm alone), for if she hadn't gotten around to cleaning it, surely I would have contrived to make that a good omen, too.

I took off my jacket, washed my hands, patted cold water across my forehead, cheeks, and eyes. Inhaled. Exhaled. Checked the time: exactly eighteen minutes before the hour. Went to the window to stare at a flying flag atop a stone tower and wondered why my belief was growing stronger and stronger that this ancient (and seemingly magical) piece of Germany was soon going to embrace me.

Time check: seven, maybe six minutes before ten o'clock.

233

I inhaled. Exhaled. Splashed still more chilled tap water across my face, leaving it there to air dry, aided and abetted by a well-directed air current of my own breath.

Five minutes before ten. It pleased me that I had, with unaccustomed foresight and efficiency, thought to synchronize my watch with the grandfather clock in the lobby. As a precaution against having fingers the temperature of chilled marble which would prove awkward in dialing, I replaced my suit jacket. Fingers, you will dial with ease. Stomach, you will resist any and all tendencies toward garrulousness.

Eyes, would you like your glasses? What for? The number is committed to memory. That's not good enough! Everything has to be checked and rechecked. There's no room here for error. Now do you want your glasses? I'm completely capable, as you must know, of reading the directory without benefit of glasses.

Inhale. Exhale. Time check: 9:58 A.M. I watched the second hand make almost imperceptible stops at each and every marking. 9:59 A.M. Inhale. Exhale. Now pick up the book. Recheck the number. And dial.

There it is! Reiker, Prof. E. C. Buhlstrasse 64 . . . 7688. See, 7688 exactly like before. Time check: ten o'clock. It's ten o'clock!

I submitted my body to the telephone with the same sense of impending oblivion that a condemned man must experience at the moment of submission to the electric chair. Ridiculous! I'm not about to die. I'm about to be born again, only this time to whom and where I belong.

Okay, I'm calm. Perfectly calm now. First for a dry run. Now reach for the first digit. Good! Good! See, not difficult.

Then after all the digits are dialed, the phone will ring. I'll hear it ring. I'll hear Mrs. Reiker lift the receiver to send out greetings to the unknown caller.

Unannounced, my heart began striking against my chest cavity with quickening regularity. It's okay. Perfectly okay. It's natural to be a little nervous now. Anybody would be. Just dial, wait until she answers, and tell her your name. Say Patricia Bergen . . . Patricia Bergen . . . Patricia Bergen. But that's only sounding somewhere within the silent cavity of your brain. Come on now, say it out loud. Say Patricia . . . Patricia.

I know very well you can do it. All I want you to do is to say audibly what you say so well in silence.

"Nooo-oh." Don't make me do what I can't do. I fell back across the bed, to wait for the spinning spiral of heat and nausea to wind down. After a while, I found I could control the dizziness by keeping my eyes focused upon the ceiling light. Shortly after that, the excess heat evaporated from my body to absorb itself into the pink fabric of my blouse.

10:18 A.M. I was able to walk (with only the slightest unsteadiness) to the bathroom where I shed jacket, blouse, and bra to wash with glycerine soap and cool water all the salt-laden perspiration from my body. By the time I had re-dressed, I understood exactly what it was that I had to do.

· 28 ·

JUST OUTSIDE the main door of the Hotel Göttingen a single black car adorned with a rooftop taxi light waited for a fare in the ice-house cold. Wait no more. You have me. We have each other. I opened the door and slid in while thrusting the opened telephone booklet in front of a slightly surprised driver. *"Buhlstrasse fier* and *sexig."*

He smiled his recognition before driving off with all the confidence that is given to those that know (or think they know) what they are doing. I sighed. Too bad I can't catch confidence like some highly communicable disease. But I don't need anybody else's, for I have my own. I settled far back into my seat to prove it.

Not until the driver turned on his windshield wipers did I realize that there was a soft snow falling on Göttingen. Sunshine and snow. I wondered . . . should I consider that as a double or only a single singularly good omen?

As the street rose, the business area gradually changed into a university area. Gothic buildings seemed to connect endlessly to other Gothic buildings via wide stone arches. Just inside one of those concrete and stone arches was the bronze likeness of a gentleman wearing nineteenth-century garb posing for the ages on a gray granite pedestal.

An unexpected snowball struck his unyielding midsection without it making any appreciable difference to either his dignity or to his position on the pedestal. A boy of eight or nine or ten, his face set off by a crimson muffler, threw his arms skyward as he jumped into the air with triumphant abandonment.

How many years had it been since another boy had taken a similarly irreverent shot at that same pompous statue?

The car made a sure but wide right-hand turn. I saw fastened to the second floor of a neat corner structure an enamel street sign, BUHLSTRASSE. Just before the end of the block, the driver pulled to the curb, pointed a nicotine-stained finger to the side window and said, *"Fier-und-sexig Buhlstrasse, fraulein."*

After the cab pulled away, I stood alone at the curb staring motionless at number 64 Buhlstrasse. I felt overwhelming awe. It was as though my religion had finally located its shrine. The house was as Anton had described it, a big house built of pale brown stone with a wide porch that wrapped itself around one half of the house, front to back.

That's where the family once gathered on balmy Sunday afternoons to discuss ethical and philosophical questions such as man's duty to God, but that was before Hitler came to power. After that Anton noted that the discussions seemed to shift somewhat more to the question of God's duty to man.

The snow that had fallen so softly against the windshield of the cab felt considerably less gentle as it struck my face. I moved up the unshoveled walk, then up the steps. Centered against the golden oak door was a weighty brass knocker, but to the left of the knob was a bell. Do I knock or do I ring? What do Germans do? Which is more polite?

The indecision began acting as a magnet, calling forth all the confused fears and conflicting needs that had for so long wrestled my obsession to an enfeebled draw.

"But nobody's going to stop me now," I said, thrusting my finger against the bell to hear a two-toned chime shatter the quiet and echo through the stillness. I prayed to God that nobody would be home while at the same time praying that everybody would be.

Then as a pinlike pain pierced my heart, I told myself that I was absolutely, positively not having a heart attack. Dr. Kopelman would never permit it! As the spasm began to subside, an unexpected click at the door sent another quick stab against a chamber of my heart.

The door was opened by a man on the upper rungs of old age. His face was thin enough, lined enough, and his facial bones visible enough to have kept Roger happily clicking away for hours. He wore dark pants, a white dress shirt open at the neck, and a rust-colored cardigan. He greeted me in a courteous tone in German, not a word of which I remotely understood.

I answered him in English, which I hoped he understood. "I wish to speak please with Mrs. Reiker."

"Ah, yes," he answered, as though he were expecting me. "Won't you please come in."

This entrance hall was bigger than almost any Jenkinsville room that I had ever seen, and if Roger's place was any criterion, than any room in Paris too. Covering the dark wood floor was an oriental rug of closely woven texture, but the design was the really interesting thing, comprised as it was of more figures and less geometrics than any of my grandmother's.

"You are here in our bleak midwinter," he said, helping me off with my coat. Right off, it struck me as strange that he would be helping me when he himself seemed so very frail that I felt as though I should be protecting him from all manner of things.

"Yes, sir," I answered. "I guess I am."

He spoke some words which were destined to be forever lost inside the closet where he had gone to hang my coat.

Over the hall table, there was a convexed mirror crowned by a carved golden eagle of great age. Even from this angle, I could see that there were many dark spots on the glass where bits of reflective silver had dried and flaked off over the years. I wanted to move directly in front of that mirror to try to determine whether age sharpens or softens images, but I didn't. The old man would notice, would think I'm vain, would think I'm primping.

He closed the closet door. "In the fireplace a wood is burning," he said, leading the way through the hall toward the back of the house.

"Yes, sir," I answered, noticing for the first time that not only had my heart attack spent itself, but my vocal chords were more or less operational. Hallelujah!

This room, which was even larger than the entrance hall, was dominated by ceiling-to-floor, wall-to-wall books, and from the leather bindings I could guess that most of them weren't even of this century. Did I know this room? I watched him remove the cast-iron fire screen to throw a couple of pine logs on the fire. Strange . . . I had never before seen this room, but still I knew it.

Of course I did! It was in this room that the war had first started for Anton. For this is the library of Professor Erikson Carl Reiker and so this would make this old man— Strange, but he seems so much older and more fragile than the father Anton had once described.

I wondered if the old man also remembers that night seventeen or eighteen years ago, back in the spring of '33. Your son remembered it. He told me how he was awakened by something; he didn't know what. But he followed the light downstairs to this very room where he found you, his father, with your head resting on that very desk.

You told your thirteen-year-old that he should go back to bed, that everything was well and that nothing was wrong, but then almost in the next breath you began speaking of your own grandfather who so many years before had been president of this very university. Pointing to the books in those mahogany cases, you said that many of them were written because your grandfather believed that a president's job was to promote scholarship and to encourage publishing.

"But our current president," you had told Anton, "with his 'let's all join the Nazis before the Nazis destroy us' mentality, would be just as comfortable burning libraries as he would be in building them."

I watched the old man carefully pull the fire screen closed before patting the backrest of a leather fireside chair. "Come sit down and warm yourself."

"Thank you, sir," I said, in unison with a mahogany mantel clock somberly chiming out the morning hour of eleven.

"She shall be coming down momentarily," he said, turning to look at the clock. "She has been teaching for three consecutive hours and by this time of day she looks forward to a cup of tea and a bit of quiet."

I rummaged through my brain for a clue to just what it was Mrs. Reiker taught. I remember Anton had spoken of her vitality, warmth, and even her beauty, but what was it she taught? Math? Foreign languages? Ballroom dancing?

As I heard myself say that I was in "no great hurry," I heard voices along with footsteps coming down the stairs. Then a dark-haired woman of about twenty-five or so entered the study followed by a somewhat younger bearded man carrying a violin case.

Right off, I tried to discover what it was that I didn't like about her. She certainly did nothing to me except frighten me by the way she displayed her superiority like a trophy. And, anyway, when was Mrs. Reiker coming down?

"Hannah, this young lady—" He turned abruptly to me. "Forgive me, but I have forgotten your name."

"Patty Bergen," I said, feeling a sharp sting of guilt for

allowing him to take responsibility for remembering a name he had never heard.

"Ah, yes, of course, Patty Bergen has been waiting to see you." Then he turned to me. "I am sorry, but I do not remember so well anymore."

I protested that "knowing me," I had neglected to introduce myself. Hannah then with exceptional presence introduced me to the departing young man whose name I heard, but never mastered. My resources were all focused on wondering if I had heard the professor right. Did he think I came this distance to see her? To see Hannah? At the door was it even remotely possible that I said "Miss" Reiker instead of Mrs. Reiker? Or is my southern pronunciation of those two words practically indistinguishable?

"You wish to speak with me?" Hannah was asking.

Why did she think I wanted to talk with her? I didn't. I only wanted to speak with her mother. With Mrs. Reiker!

Hannah looked at me in a way I didn't like. In a way that suggested I needed prompting. "You are interested," she was asking, "in studying the violin?"

Why don't I just say it? Say that there's been some misunderstanding. Say that I know it's been completely my fault, but may I please speak with your mother. May I please speak with your mother is the only thing I have to say. And what is so unspeakably frightening about that?

"I'm sorry for any misunderstanding that I may have caused," I heard myself say. "But I came here today to speak with your mother . . . Mrs. Reiker."

Hannah looked as though she had been given a shaking. I turned to look at the old man in time to see him seem to crunch forward and inward, but it was Hannah who spoke.

"My mother is dead. She died of a stroke last June." She had moved to her father's side to lay her hand across his wrist. "I regret having to inform you of this."

"Oh," I said, trying to make some sense of Hannah's words. For some reason, I saw that bronze statue which had been struck midsection how many times? By how many snowballs? And for how many years? Does there ever come a point when even the invincible will crumble from the cumulative effect of too many snowballs?

I turned back toward Hannah and the old man and I could see that they were both, in somewhat different ways, struggling to right themselves. This is not my fault. Not one bit my fault. Grief this great is just like any other combustible. Sure, sure it is, but who asked me to go running around waving a blazing torch? I simply can't do this to them. Simply cannot place them under any more stress.

I took a step toward them and then I took another step. "I'm so very sorry," I told them, as I searched for eye contact. Then I said goodbye as I walked from the library back into the great hall.

Instantly the old man was behind me, taking my coat from a wooden hanger and saying that the next time I am in the neighborhood he would be honored to have me visit.

That's when it struck me that my being here had some significance for him, too. I took his hand. "I don't know if I'll ever again be in this neighborhood." But I had to avoid his eyes, had to avoid seeing the sorrow that I knew was there.

"My wife would have liked you."

" . . . Your wife would have liked . . . me?"

"She brought many foreign students, English-speaking

243

students like you to our home, but, of course, she liked some more than others."

"Yes," I answered, far more interested in learning why Mrs. Reiker would have liked me than in correcting the professor's assumption that I was a student.

But his head moved in a sudden way that indicated he was already off on another tack. "Please kindly tell them all at the English-speaking alliance . . . " He stared down at the rug as though he too had just become fascinated by the lack of geometrics. " . . . not to send any more students to *fier-und-sexig Buhlstrasse*. Tell them please that Frau Deborah Reiker is dead."

Without warning, I found myself embracing him, trying to give him the comfort of a moment of closeness. Then quickly and wordlessly, I broke away. Out the door, down the unshoveled walk and into the street. I moved quickly along the curb, demanding that my brain and body be consumed by both the exertion and the concentration of an unaccustomed run.

· 29 ·

WHEN I ENTERED room 515 of the Hotel Göttingen, my breath was as shallow as it was quick, and my forehead, in spite of the freezing outside temperature, sprouted miniature bubbles of perspiration. I dropped my coat and my jacket on the bed, and kicked off my shoes before pulling a train schedule from the satin side pocket of my suitcase. Ah, yes, here it is: A train leaves Göttingen at 4:10 P.M. arriving in Paris at 10:55 P.M.

I figured that I had time for both a bath and a nap. The bath might thoroughly cleanse me, but I doubt if a two-hour sleep could even begin to penetrate the depth of my fatigue.

Behind the hotel's large front desk was a black-suited man who looked as though he had been trained since infancy to provide impeccable service to others. After placing a key inside a numbered cubby, he greeted me. "Fraulein?"

"*Finif-eins-finif,*" I said, sliding my room key across the dark marble-topped counter. "I'm checking out now. May I have my bill, please?"

He nodded ritualistically before entering a small connecting office. When he returned, he produced a statement embossed at the top with a tricolored coat of arms. That was the first thing that struck me. The second thing was the balance which came within a very few marks of decimating all that was left of my worldly wealth. The bill came to roughly twice the balance that I had estimated.

Then just before panic overtook me, I caught the error. "Sir, there's a mistake on this bill." I pointed to the offending line. "You have charged me for two nights, but I have only been here *one* night."

For a few moments he bent low over the statement before returning upright to point with his entire hand to the old Roman numeraled clock behind the desk. "I regret that there is no mistake, fraulein. The hotel's check-out time is eleven o'clock which you have exceeded by more than four hours. Therefore we are required to bill you for an additional night."

"Well, I didn't know that! Why wasn't I told that?"

"You were, fraulein. The information is so posted inside each chamber. The inside door of each chamber."

"Yes, well, but not everybody can read German—it's not a very popular language, you know."

"Our sign is posted in four languages, fraulein. German, French, Italian, *and* English."

"Well, I certainly didn't see—at least, I didn't notice your sign, honest!"

"Nevertheless."

"Nevertheless what?"

"Nevertheless I am still required to bill you for the second night."

I tried to think, but I couldn't—the ancient mahogany clock's strident, every-second sounding was interfering with my thoughts.

"Required to do it?"

He nodded smartly. "Required policy of the Hotel Göttingen. Those are my orders."

Not only were the clock sounds harshly metallic, but its carvings were grotesque. Like so many severed heads captured in wood at the moment of beheading.

"What did you say?"

"I said, fraulein, that I am only following the orders of the management."

"Following orders? . . . That's what she said you'd say."

"Beg your pardon?"

" . . . Told me that at The Skyway one day . . . said you people didn't care about wrong . . . didn't care about right. Only orders . . . said you all were very big on following orders. I didn't understand then, Grandmother, but

I understand now. And you were right! Germans take orders from anybody—a young waiter wearing gold braid on his red jacket!"

"Fraulein, this is no conversa——"

"I want to ask you about that waiter—he wasn't really a waiter, only an acne-faced busboy wearing a red jacket. If he told you to find Jews, you'd be real quick to run out and do that, now wouldn't you?"

"Pay your bill and kindly leave this hotel!"

"You are the taker of orders, not me! That's what you told everybody at Nuremburg. I was only taking orders. You remember saying, I was only taking orders?"

"Fraulein, please. You are causing a disturbance."

"Please? Are you begging me? Toby, Miera, their husbands and all of their children gone. And all you can say is please . . . PLEASE!"

"Stop that! I'm telling you. Keep your voice down. Our guests require quiet."

"What do I care about your guests! I don't care about your guests! I care about Judah. I care about who gave the order to find Jews! And just who was it that gave the order to behead Judah?"

"Please, please. People are watching. I will telephone the manager . . . maybe an exception." He backed into the connecting office, slamming the door behind him.

"COME BACK HERE!" I screamed at the door which I heard being bolted from the inside. "COME BACK HERE, DAMN YOU, AND TELL ME WHO MURDERED THEM!"

But when the only answer that came back was the mocking *tsk, tsk, tsk* of the severed-head clock, I picked up the heavy desk inkwell, and with all the strength of inflamed self-righteousness, sent it crashing through that plate glass face. I watched with freshly liberated enjoyment as thick globs of black ink streamed downward to totally obliterate numeral VI.

I lay on my back on a long hard bench and thought how strange it is that the Germans have just as lousy jails as the Arkansans. With all that experience the Germans have had incarcerating people (not to mention all those final solutions) wouldn't you think that they'd have learned how to run a really good jail by now?

But if I wanted to be completely fair about it (and I don't believe that I did), I'd note that besides this bench, there is also a cot covered with a brick-colored expanse of rubber sheeting. I wondered if the sheeting was there to keep the mattress clean or was it there because it was already filthy. I averted my eyes because I didn't like the idea of knowing for certain.

Metal struck metal with enough force to startle a reaction from within me. I looked on the other side of the bars to see a cop with enough gold braid on his shoulders to impress the Gestapo.

"Fraulein, we have located among your possessions a return railroad ticket to Paris."

Someday I'm going to have to learn how to respond to a statement that tells me exactly what it is that I already know. In Jenkinsville, folks are all the time saying, "You shore can say that again," or for a little variety, "Now, ain't

249

that the living gospel," but somehow both of those phrases seem more appropriate to Jenkinsville than they do to Göttingen.

"There is a late afternoon train to Paris, fraulein. Would you care to be on the 4:10?"

Who knows what I want? Or, in fact, did I want anything? Or did I want nothing? Nothing to hurt, nothing to be taken away. Not ever. Maybe nothing is too big a deal and way too much to ask for, anyway. But will somebody please tell me what's a person to do when they're too afraid of life to live and too afraid of death to die?

Another metallic rap for attention. He's got to stop that! Can't he tell that I've just had all my skin surgically removed? I think that must be why I hurt so much. Not having skin. But maybe it didn't happen surgically. No, I think maybe I was born that way. Think I'll write myself up in *The Journal of the American Medical Association,* and then Kopelman and all the others will understand, once and for all, about this birth defect of mine which permits exposed tissue to remain at the mercy of merciless elements.

"The train for Paris leaves in twenty-five minutes, fraulein." The cop dropped a hefty ring of keys from one hand to the other. "I will personally take you to the railroad station if you promise to behave decently."

I heard myself laughing, but it wasn't anything like the inspired laughter that I once shared with Ruth and Anton and later with Roger. My laugh sounded unnatural, as though it had been recorded many years earlier, and was now being replayed on an ancient gramophone.

I raised myself from the bench to walk with inordinate

slowness to where the bars separated us. "You have no right to speak to me of decency," I told him in a voice that resembled a hoarse whisper. "No right at all, for I am a Jew and you . . . you're only a German."

· 30 ·

As THE TRAIN took a wide-angled, around-the-bend turn, I caught my first returning glimpse of Paris. On the other side of the darkness, it shone like an unclaimed treasure. Paris glitters and Göttingen doesn't. Even so, that isn't the essential difference between the two cities.

Because for all of Paris's glamor it's still a city that doesn't spend a lot of time fooling around with pretend. So that's it! The quality that I've admired both in this city and in Roger. The city and the man both have the strength to take life on an "as is" basis.

Much more "as is" strength here than in Jenkinsville, where people pull the gospel so tight around themselves that they squeeze out life along with the devil.

While you, Göttingen, with your feudal architecture, are no better. Medieval towers and ancient forts encouraged and nurtured my belief in all those things, which I see now, could never be. At first, I believed that I had at last found a place where a damsel's distress would be invariably short-lived and princesses and paupers would not only be expected to prevail, but live happily ever after.

At Gare St. Lazare, my seat mate Raoul, a lawyer on his way back home to Madrid, carried both my suitcases out of the station and onto the sidewalk. Actually, it was Raoul's second very needed favor to me. And I'm pretty certain that he didn't realize it because if you wear good clothes, nobody would ever guess you could be going hungry.

Shortly after leaving Göttingen my ulcer gnawed a sharp reminder to put food into my stomach and as much as I wanted to soothe the angry little beast, I knew that I had enough money for cab fare and I maybe had enough money for a dining car dinner, but not for both. Definitely not for both!

As I with growing concern considered my dwindling choices, a tall man of at least forty, with solid gold cufflinks and a perfectly enormous Adam's apple, appeared before me to ask (in French yet!) if the seat next to me were taken. I must have smiled very welcomingly because his words came through to me as clearly as if he were saying, "Dinner will soon be served."

And I might have continued smiling too for many more moments than necessary because that's when it struck me that in spite of Göttingen and my inability (or unwillingness) to even think about what happened there, my dedication to my own personal survival seemed pretty much intact.

While the taxi waited (and I worried that the meter might be running), Raoul with maddening leisure placed his vellum calling card in my hand and offered me the back of another to write my own address. With considerable reluctance, I wrote: Patty Bergen, Jenkinsville, Arkansas, U.S.A. Then we shook hands and said our goodbyes.

As the cab wound adroitly through the traffic, I wondered at the size of the scandal if this oversized, overaged Spaniard should ever decide to present himself in my home town.

At number 39 Place St. Sulpice, I told the driver to pull over in front of the still lively Café Jacques because just three flights up is (has got to be) home. The fare was 220 francs. I slipped the last of my money—three 100 franc notes—out of my wallet. Told the driver to kindly carry my luggage up to the top of the stairs and in my last act of solvency told him to keep the change.

As I climbed the stairs, one fatigued foot following another, the cabby passed me on his fast trot back down with a smile, a wave, and a "Bonsoir, mademoiselle."

When I reached the paint-chipped door to our—to Roger's —place, I stood, trying to breathe in the air that would inflate my rapidly deflating supply of courage. And maybe even in shorter supply than courage was conviction. I didn't know what to show Roger, my love or my anger.

Who gave him the right to hurl those terrible accusations at me? I'd like to give him one good sudden swift kick and then I would no longer be angry with him. I would have made him suffer at least a little of what he had made me suffer. We would call it a draw. Then who knows, we might be able to love to the finish.

I wanted to be at peace with Roger again and, even more urgently than that, I had to rest. And it was for that reason that I knocked.

That's when I heard a sound (a feminine-gender sound of lovemaking interrupted?) on the other side of the door. I wondered if my spent body could make it unseen down the steps without having to come face-to-face with either of them. Damn her! Damn him! And damn the French! That's all they ever do. That's all they ever think of!

Suddenly I conceived a very clear picture of just what it is that French Catholics whisper to their priests once inside those mysterious closetlike cubicles. "Tell me, Father, is the church positive, I mean really positive about the existence of sex in the afterlife?"

The door opened a wedge and Roger, not surprisingly, seemed surprised. Even so, he invited me in. What a really stupid thing to do.

"Thanks, anyway! But I don't want to meet her. It was only that I happened to be in the neighborhood and thought I'd say hello. But I'm already late for an appointment, so hello and goodbye," I heard myself say, while wondering where it is that I could possibly find to go.

He wore a mocking half-smile on his lips. "Meet her?" He swung the door back, allowing a full unobstructed view of the nobody-there interior.

"You are hearing with jealous ears, my friend."

"Maybe," I said, not allowing myself to become completely

255

convinced until I saw a single glass of well-sipped burgundy on the table. "But it is you, *mon ami,* who speaks with a cruel and jealous tongue."

"Yes, well, perhaps, but I deserved better treatment than you dispensed, dear lady. Every day I came to the hospital, yes? I count the days until we can be together again. Yes, it's true. I'm like a crazy man counting the days. And you! What is it you do? At the last moment and under the most direct questioning, you finally admit that you're not coming home. That you never had any intention—"

"Roger, it wasn't nearly as premeditated as you're trying to make it sound. Olivia Marcou made me realize that I simply could not leave this continent without doing what it was that I came here to do. I had to go. My obsession demanded it!"

"Well, I was taught that common courtesy demands that even a hotel reservation be cancelled, but did you?"

"No, but I wish that I had. I'm tired. I'm sorry, but I'm so very tired."

Roger ceased the enumeration of my transgressions to look at me with unguarded vision. *"Mon Dieu, tu es fatiguée!"*

"I'm more than tired. I want to retreat undisturbed, at least for a while, into a novocained existence."

As he helped me off with my coat, he asked where my other things were. My suitcases?

I pointed toward the stairs and with barely a nod, he went after them. When he reappeared at the doorway with a suitcase in each hand, he asked, "Shall I hang up your clothes?"

"Don't bother," I told him. "They need your concern a lot less than I do."

As he moved, his eyes seemed to fix upon me as though

I were a navigational chart and he was afraid of losing his way. I patted the space next to me on the sofabed. "Come, Roger, sit here. I'll tell you some things that you'll like to hear."

Obedient as a schoolboy, he did as he was told. Then he placed his hands in his lap and stared at them as if attempting to understand a strange and unfathomable entity.

I brought him to me, stroking his face with my fingertips. Gradually, I felt his tension ease. He was submitting to me because only I had the power to make all the bad go away. Shoo! Oh, God, Roger, I wish, I really wish I could do that for you. I'll try to do that for you.

"What I did that was wrong," I told him, "I'm very sorry about. But you must never think that it was because I didn't care for you. Because as much as I know how to love, Roger, I love you."

· 31 ·

THE PARIS MORNING that woke me was periwinkle blue. A diffused light caught the high points of his face, especially the forehead and cheeks, with a cool lucent quality. And that's when it came to me that if I were the photographer, I'd know exactly what I wanted to photograph and why.

My hand made a crescent sweep across Roger's warm bare back and I got to wondering if something can still have value even if it lasts for only a little while. He pressed toward me as a small boat might wash gently against its moorings. I answered my own question: Longevity can't be the only test of love.

Then it wasn't true what I had feared. After Germany I felt far too splintered to ever again, on my own volition, give anything away. From me there'd be no pennies to the poor or bread to the hungry or words of cheer to the lonely. I couldn't possibly give anything away because, as it was, there was already too little left that was me.

With you, Roger, I don't think it was like that. At least with you I still had something to give, didn't I? And funny thing is, I have felt neither depleted nor deprived for the experience.

At the same time the bells of St. Sulpice began solemnly stroking out the morning hour of eight, Roger and I strolled into Jacques's café. The oversized espresso machine emitted soft, throaty sounds while the pungent smell of the coffee seemed as reassuring as a small-town scene painted by Norman Rockwell.

As soon as Jacques spotted me, he rushed from behind the counter, welcoming me with "Encore à la café du Jacques, et encore à votre santé!" He wiped his hands on his morning-fresh, around-the-belly white apron before offering them to me. Even after I assured him under direct questioning that I was beginning to feel good again, he told me that to feel good again it was absolutely necessary for me to regain my lost weight.

Roger and I slid in next to each other at a window table and although we were acutely alert to one another's presence, neither of us broke our mutually cherished habit of morning silence. He read *Le Monde* while sipping espresso and I sipped Jacques's steaming café au lait while watching chilled pedestrians walk with long quick strides down Place St. Sulpice.

After a while, I stopped staring at the Parisians and he stopped reading the newspaper. "We didn't talk much last night," he said. "You haven't as yet mentioned your trip. Was Germany everything you hoped for?"

"Not what I hoped for, no. I was seven months late. Mrs. Reiker died in June."

"Oh," he said, covering my hand with his own. And I wondered if we had ever achieved more intimacy than now. It was true, and yet how could that be? Handholding is still primary-grade stuff. And in these months hadn't we shared our bodies and our beds? A lot of external visions and a few internal fears? Now our possession-in-common is only a moment of shared sorrow.

"Roger, I want you to know how I feel," I told him, while emotionally rushing from the scene. "Only . . . I can't talk about it . . . not yet."

Leaning his head back, he closed his eyes without releasing my hand. "I think I can guess how you feel. It must feel something like being forced to climb an unscalable mountain. Ignoring cold, hunger, and fatigue to continue that ascent to the very summit. Only to discover, once you get there, that it's all been for nothing. Because there is nothing there for you."

" . . . nothing there for me?"

Roger looked enormously surprised. "Was there? Something?"

I heard myself sigh. "I guess not. I don't know! Maybe."

"So you did," said Roger, breaking into an I-caught-you grin, "find something there, didn't you?"

I breathed in deep enough to activate what energy I had. "Only that I could do it. That I, surprisingly actually, had the strength to do it. Also there was that view from the heights. That's when I saw—clearly saw—that there was more than one mountain in my life. Some could be seen and some couldn't be, but just the same, they were all out there. All out there waiting for me.

"But what was climbed was already climbed, and I understand now that I'll never have to chase that vision or scale that particular mountain again."

Bette Greene, who is celebrated for the strong emotional response that readers have to her books, was born in a small Arkansas town. Later she lived in Memphis, Tennessee, and Paris, France. She now lives in Brookline, Massachusetts, with her husband.

Summer of My German Soldier, the companion novel to *Morning Is a Long Time Coming*, was an ALA Notable Book, a National Book Award finalist, and a 1973 *New York Times* Outstanding Book of the Year, and has become a modern classic. Her other novels published in Puffin are *Philip Hall Likes Me. I Reckon Maybe.*, a 1973 Newbery Honor Book and a 1974 *New York Times* Outstanding Book of the Year, and *Get On Out of Here, Philip Hall.*